~ Promise Ring ~

by Tony C. Anderson

~ February 26, 2006 ~

Note for Librarians: A cataloguing record for this book is available from Library and Archives Canada at www.collectionscanada.ca/amicus/index-e.html

ISBN 1-4120-8978-6

Printed in Victoria, BC, Canada. Printed on paper with minimum 30% recycled fibre. Trafford's print shop runs on "green energy" from solar, wind and other environmentally-friendly power sources.

TRAFFORD
PUBLISHING™

Offices in Canada, USA, Ireland and UK

Book sales for North America and international:
Trafford Publishing, 6E–2333 Government St.,
Victoria, BC V8T 4P4 CANADA
phone 250 383 6864 (toll-free 1 888 232 4444)
fax 250 383 6804; email to orders@trafford.com

Book sales in Europe:
Trafford Publishing (UK) Limited, 9 Park End Street, 2nd Floor
Oxford, UK OX1 1HH UNITED KINGDOM
phone 44 (0)1865 722 113 (local rate 0845 230 9601)
facsimile 44 (0)1865 722 868; info.uk@trafford.com

Order online at:
trafford.com/06-0734

10   9   8   7   6   5   4   3   2

~ Thanks to Sally Gunn for typing and editing, not only this book, but the last one. For Brad's baby Isaiah and my sister Sara's baby Kaylea, but not to read, not until they're a lot older. ~

Also by Tony C. Anderson:

Understanding the Afterlife

Table of Contents

Chapter One

A Faceless Man

Walking into the city of Kodaya, a fourth of a mile from the castle, Queen Amelia was strolling through the main street. Going past the merchants selling everything from clothes to food. Moving past the many people who were selling things or pointless junk they don't need, like they always do. As she went by, a few older people shouted at the top of their lungs, "Everyone, it's Queen Amelia!"

"Away from me! I don't have time for your fame! I'm strictly on business today – I have a slave to sell!" Amelia shouted back angrily, raising her arms as she pushed the bearded slave in front of her. She was holding onto a chain attached to a metal leash around his neck, like a dog collar. Amelia pushed him forward by kicking him into the dirt. After falling down on the hard ground, he got up, groaning and covered in dirt.

"But Amelia," called a younger woman near her, "we haven't seen you in a long time!" Amelia moved through the crowd, ignoring the woman's plea for attention. She had a look on her face like, see if I give a care.

Eventually, she reached the man she was seeking, the slave buyer. "So what do you have for today that you want to get off your hands?" the buyer asked Amelia.

"Whatever I care to sell," Amelia answered flippantly.

"You know, I never liked your attitude," the buyer responded, glaring over towards Amelia.

"You know what? I really don't care what you think of me," Amelia commented carelessly. Leaning towards the buyer, she asked, "So now, do you want him or not?"

"Fine – here's your money," the buyer replied, as he handed her fifty gold coins in a pouch.

"Thanks – it was nice not doing business with you," she answered, sarcasm dripping from her words as she handed him the key to the metal collar.

The buyer grabbed the chain and key. He gave the chain a jerk as he looked over at the silent, bearded slave and smiled chillingly. "You're coming with me now."

"Don't let him get away," Amelia called over her shoulder as she turned to walk back to the castle, the gold coins held firmly in her hands.

"I won't. I've got plenty of work for him to do," the buyer called back.

Five years then passed.

Chapter Two

Bedtime

It was dark outside, very dark. These truly are the Dark Ages. The large castle's drawbridge was up. These were definitely the medieval times. Within the windows of this castle, past the deep-blue-velvet curtains were the rooms of Queen Amelia and her daughter, Dorkla. Amelia looked outside her window to see the foam-like fog rolling over the waters surrounding the castle.

With a sigh, she pulled the curtains closed, then headed toward her bed to call it a night. Before she reached it, however, Amelia could hear Dorkla yelling, "Mommy, Mommy, come quick!" At her daughter's call, Amelia headed out of her room and proceeded up the stairs to Dorkla's room, holding a candle in front of her to light her way. Amelia sighed, as she knew it was just one of her typical temper tantrums she would usually throw.

"Just hold on, I'm coming, dear," Amelia called out to her daughter. The candle gave off a small, flickering light that reflected onto the gray walls. Apparently, the past has been very hard for Dorkla. Amelia had told her that her dad, King Davia, passed away from an unknown illness and that he died quickly because she had put a deadly curse on him. Children will believe anything you tell them, Amelia thought to herself. Plus unbeknownst to Dorkla, Amelia wanted all the money and treasure gained from collecting taxes of the villages. Reaching Dorkla's room, she saw her daughter's anxious face. "So what is it, especially at this time of night, my loving child?" Amelia asked in a soothing tone.

"Well, I just thought maybe I saw a ghost, Mother," Dorkla whispered fearfully, trembling nervously.

Sitting down on Dorkla's bed and putting her arm around her, Amelia asked in a puzzled tone, "What are you talking about? You know there's no such thing as ghosts!"

Dorkla answered in a frightened tone, "Well, if it wasn't a ghost, then maybe there was a big, scary monster under my bed."

"Now, don't speak such nonsense and go to sleep!" Amelia stated abruptly.

Dorkla crept back under the covers and asked in a little voice, "Okay, then will you tuck me in, Mommy, please?" Amelia gently pulled the blanket over her daughter and kissed her cheek. Dorkla looked up at her. "Mommy, what do you think Father is doing in Heaven?" she inquired.

Amelia smiled at her. "Honey, I'm sure he's smiling down at you, glad to see how beautiful you've become," she answered in a loving tone. She then arose from Dorkla's bed and returned to her room so she could go and get some sleep herself.

As Amelia finally crawled into her own bed, she breathed a sigh, not of relief but of despair. After lying there for what seemed to be a very long time, she drifted off into slumber. The night then slowly passed and trickled into daylight at the rising sun of morning.

Around the wooden table in the castle's kitchen, Amelia was bustling about making a typical breakfast – some eggs, bread and some fruit juice made the day before. Most of the food they ate was made from and harvested by the village store. In exchange for payment of food, Amelia paid with money from the taxes she earned as their queen. Not exactly fair business, she thought to herself, but it worked for her.

Chapter Three

Sunday Mourning

It was at this time Dorkla came down the staircase to eat breakfast. As she sat down, she found herself next to Amelia, who was talking to herself. "For so many years, I've been queen of my kingdom, and for what? I don't seem to get any respect."

Dorkla tried to cut in on her mother's reverie. "Who doesn't give you any respect, Mother?"

Dorkla's words seemed to snap her mother back to the present time. "Never mind me, Dorkla," Amelia replied, "just go ahead and eat your eggs. They're getting warm."

Dorkla looked puzzled as she tried to gently correct her mother. "What are you talking about, Mother? Don't you mean cold?" Changing the subject, she asked Amelia, "Mom, how old are you and how old will be when you die?"

"Well, I'm 33 years old. How old are you? So act your age and not your shoe size," Amelia snapped. "And death – how would I know? Do I look like a psychic? If so, then let me ask my crystal ball!"

Dorkla looked even more puzzled. "What are you talking about, Mother? You don't even have a crystal ball!"

Amelia sighed in exasperation. "I don't mean it literally; it's a figure of speech, like break a leg."

As Dorkla fell silent and began to eat, she wondered to herself about her father being dead. Looking up at Amelia, she asked, "Mother, how and when did Father die? I was very young and I don't remember it happening."

"I don't feel like talking about that right now," Amelia began, but seeing her daughter's face looking crestfallen, she added, "but after you're done eating, we'll visit your father's grave, okay?"

"All right," Dorkla replied, brightening a little. After breakfast was done, Dorkla ran and fetched her long black cloak, and they headed out the castle towards the site, which was on the castle grounds. Dorkla held her mother's hand while they strolled out of the castle so she wouldn't stray, even though deep down inside she wanted to.

The sun's rays were beaming down through the clouds as they made their way along the path behind the castle to see her father's tombstone. It wasn't a real tombstone, actually – it was more like a rock with absolutely no words carved into it. Although a commonplace occurrence, it still had to be rather creepy having any sort of graveyard behind your home, whether it be your dead dog, cat or goldfish.

As they neared what was believed to be King Davia's grave, Dorkla approached it and knelt down near the rock. A small handful of dried-out wildflowers were leaning against it, placed there by Dorkla several days ago. "Oh, Father, I so wished you didn't die!" Dorkla cried out. "Because I never got to see or get the chance to say good-bye. If only I could have seen you, given you a hug or had you hold me in your arms and then sit on your lap. If only for a moment more." She looked as if she would cry, but she slowly arose, still gazing at the rock as if mesmerized.

Amelia's voice cut through her veil of sadness. "That sounds about good enough. Now I have some of my own words of wisdom. From ashes to ashes, fallen to dust. He never cared about any of us. A forgotten man whose life will remain within the sand. The time has come to bid farewell and Amen," Amelia quoted bitterly. As she was speaking, she picked up a small handful of dirt and was letting it slowly trickle from her hand.

"That's not right to say, and you know it's not true, Mother!" Dorkla lashed out.

Amelia seized hold of Dorkla's hand and retorted, "I think I've made my point. Now let's get going."

At times like this, Dorkla wondered as they hurried back down the path towards the castle door, if Amelia even really cared about her father at all, and she also largely couldn't understand why they got married in the first place.

Dorkla reflected that maybe by being somewhat alone, living in a castle with only Dorkla for companionship had driven Amelia crazy over time. Besides, she had heard that those who usually live in castles have their own court jesters to make them laugh, guards to protect them and other people to live with or visit them.

Amelia decided that once back inside the castle, she needed to go and get her money. By that point, Dorkla was more than sick of holding onto her mother's hand every step on the way in life. She just wanted to get away from the castle and eventually make some friends or to do something with her life, to somehow not always feel confined by these four kingdom walls. She was so sick of being under Queen Meanie's authority, always having to be bossing her around.

After Amelia retrieved her money, they headed to the shops within Kodaya City to pick up some things. Amelia had a firm grip on Dorkla, dragging her behind her as opposed to possibly leaving her able to run away.

Once in Kodaya City, Amelia busied herself purchasing milk and a large quantity of eggs. Dorkla looked glumly at the eggs. They were precisely the exact food she despised the most, mainly because they ate them at almost every morning meal. Also sometimes for the noon meal and dinner. They would eat them so often that they might just as well buy their own chickens to lay eggs for them.

While Amelia's back was turned, Dorkla began sneaking peeks at the finished clothing that was for sale not far from the edible items, made by a local tailor and brought here to be sold. A very pretty red gown on a frame caught her eye. It was made of elegant red velvet. It had an Empire waist, long flared sleeves, and delicate lace trim in black and white, as were the styles of the times. Even though she knew her mother wouldn't possibly get it for her, since Amelia seldom purchased anything for her at all. But as Dorkla couldn't stop thinking of the beautiful gown, she thought that she might as well ask her. It couldn't hurt, could it? she thought to herself. Dorkla gathered up the strength to approach Amelia and ask in a sweet voice, "Mother, can you please buy me this dress? It's really pretty!" She tugged on Amelia's hand and gently touched the beautiful scarlet dress.

Chapter Four

Birthday Party

"You know I can't possibly afford that, especially for you," Amelia protested. "What do you really think, I'm made of money? It doesn't grow on bushes, you know!"

"Don't you mean trees, Mother?" Dorkla asked as sweetly as she could muster, correcting her mother once again.

Amelia's face darkened in anger. "You think you know about everything, don't you?" she hissed angrily. "But you know what, you're just a stupid child. You don't know anything yet. Because I've been on this wretched earth a lot longer than you!"

"But that doesn't make you smarter," Dorkla replied. "So can I have it – please, Mother?" changing the subject, hoping she would forget and feel sorry for her.

"I may think about it, possibly. Maybe. For your eighth birthday tomorrow," Amelia responded.

Hearing Amelia's hopefulness, Dorkla tried to get all she could get from her. "Really? Can I have a party with clowns and friends?" she asked, getting excited to hear her mother's response.

"No way, little lady! You should just be glad that I don't ground you for the way you backtalked me. Just be thankful I'm buying you a dress and a cake. Besides, you don't even have any friends," Amelia retorted.

Dorkla looked at her mother defiantly. "It's because you don't let me have any. You keep me trapped at home. God forbid that I get any fresh air. And wow, Mother, you're really going all out this year. Normally you would just give me more candles. I'm very surprised that I haven't burned down the whole castle by now," she stated in a sarcastic tone.

To Dorkla's surprise, Amelia appeared thoughtful. "I guess you're right. I am a little overprotective, but that's just because I don't want to see you get hurt."

By this time, Amelia was getting ready to leave the shop, as she'd purchased all the things she'd needed and paid for. Since there weren't many people outside today, Amelia didn't have to worry about being hounded by a crowd.

Back at the castle, they had their noon meal, which consisted of egg sandwiches and milk. In between bites, Dorkla sparked a conversation about things, Amelia despised discussing.

Chapter Five

Religious Conversation

"Mother," Dorkla began, "why don't we go to church at all? Isn't God going to think that we don't believe in Him?"

Amelia thought a minute before answering. "What does believing in possibly have anything to do with going to church? It's just visiting a building every single Sunday. It's not at what faith and belief is. Because it's within your heart where it really resides." It wasn't that Amelia didn't believe. It's just she sometimes was very skeptical of her own faith and had gone through times of doubt now and then just as any other believer would.

Amelia looked at her daughter steadily as she continued. "Plus, how do you expect me to even to spend time worshipping a god I couldn't possibly see at all? A god who doesn't even show Himself to His own very people He created, though He was seen, they say a long time ago by a few people."

"By who?" Dorkla asked.

"I think it was Adam and Eve, plus Moses and maybe some other people," Amelia replied, "but I'm not sure. If we were so-called made in the image of God, the supposed to be face of God, then couldn't we just look in the river or at each other to know what God looks like?"

"But I – I've never seen what God looks like," Dorkla admitted.

"Exactly!" Amelia snapped. "So how can you believe in Him so much? Am I supposed to be led to believe that some history books filled with the things that happened a long time ago are more important than what happens now? So why isn't any of that book I've heard about - The Bible - being written today? It's like saying that back then is more important than these days."

Amelia paused to catch her breath, then continued in her ranting. "So where is God? Is He just hiding from me for no apparent reason? It's funny, isn't it? God expects you to rely on Him, but instead He wants to remain invisible to the naked eye. Oh, and the world's going to end – isn't that just dandy? Well, why is it taking so awfully long then? People have been telling me when I was young that the world was ending, but I'm still waiting. How did they write The Bible? Didn't you ever wonder about that?"

Dorkla was taken aback by her mother's tirade. "No," she answered slowly, "I never ever really gave it much thought, actually."

"Well, maybe you should," Amelia replied. "They say that The Bible's the greatest book ever written, but how can it be? I'm not saying that it's not a good book – it is, that's for sure. But it was written by so many authors, not that I'm questioning its authenticity or anything. It just contains so many books, if you were to include what they completely wrote. So shouldn't it be the greatest books of all time. Also, how could they write about the beginning of time or the end of time, for that matter, when they weren't even there? Plus, how did they write about all those people? Did they just follow everyone around with paper, writing everything down that they said like some sort of secretary would? What if they didn't write it all down exactly like everything they really said or did?"

Dorkla tried to answer all of her questions with just one suggested answer. "But God told them, Mother, so it must and has to be correct."

Amelia gave her daughter a contemptuous look. "That's just completely plain ignorant and really closemindedly stupid. So please, get real! All of The Bible was written by man, and the rest of it what was written that God or Jesus had apparently spoken to them. I'm sorry, but I just think that The Bible sometimes contradicts itself over and over. One of the Ten Commandments says 'Thou shall not kill.' Yet even in The Bible, people just go around murdering other people left and right and then some and even, if you can you believe this, be given praise for it. Also, they praise God, what I thought long ago was the One who told them not to murder. I wonder, how do they justify their murderous actions? I'm guessing they didn't – they probably just claimed, "Oh, the Devil made me do it.""

Dorkla interrupted to speak her mind. "What people are you referring to when you said they killed, Mother?"

Amelia answered, "Well, there's David, who of course slew Goliath. Then there would be Samson, who killed many people with a jawbone of an ass, not to mention all of the lions he also murdered. Plus there were a lot of people who fought in wars for God. Also, people publicly stoned others back then and still do for adultery. It might say don't be angry, yet it's just plain perfectly all right for God to be. Give me a break – what does God have to be angry about? He created us – let there be a Devil and the choice to sin. So it's our fault that two people out of the whole human race messed up? We're to blame because some people we never met ate an apple, peach, or some other fruit that probably tasted the same as the ones on the other tree. Didn't you ever notice The Bible is more full of 'do-nots' than it does 'do's'? Most of the book never tells you what you can do. But that was back then. Am I supposed to be following the rules of long ago or now?"

Dorkla interrupted her mother's speech once again. "But all you have to do is just have faith."

Amelia looked angry again. "What, so I can walk on water? I can't, and I have never seen anyone else do so. Am I just supposed to take all of this literally? You know that I've never been able to turn my water into wine. If I try to be completely perfect and follow all of The Bible's rules, I would never be able to keep up. These are the questions I've had since I was young going to church and stayed with me my entire life since. For what – so I could go back home and live with my atheist parents?"

Chapter Six

Amelia's Diary

"I don't really have any more need for religion, and I'm just plain sick of hearing about it," Amelia stated flatly, wanting to end this discussion.

"But isn't it about a relationship with Jesus Christ, not religion?" Dorkla persisted. "How will I know if I don't explore and search for myself?"

"Looking for what?" Amelia asked wearily. "To try to find out who may be right or wrong? Only to waste your whole life away to find out what you could have found out at the very beginning?" Amelia looked around the room, hoping to find something, anything, to spark another topic of discussion.

Dorkla looked at her mother, more puzzled than ever. "Are you saying that if I go looking for God that it is a waste of time?" she asked.

Amelia heaved a long sigh before answering. "No, I'm not saying that. If you do find God, it will be when you finally die. Otherwise, I have to say that you're just plain searching for thin air. You know, when I went to church, they never told me about accepting some Christ but just to be good to everyone, and that's about it. I'd rather have something tangible in my life, and I don't mean a stupid rosary necklace of beads. That's why I think that the church has made itself idols and has become full of pride in the process. They try to make me think that I can't believe in God because of the way I dress and all sorts of things that don't even really matter at all. They enjoy judging me left and right. So where's the love at?"

Dorkla looked affectionately at her mother. "But I love you, Mother," she said softly.

Amelia leaned over and hugged Dorkla. "Thank you," she replied in a gentle tone.

After releasing her and leaning back, Dorkla whispered, "You're not taking life for granted, are you, Mother?"

"Not at all," Amelia answered. "You know, I live my life my way, the best way I can every day. Trying to enjoy every moment, know that I could just as well die any day now. So now," she added, pushing herself away from the table and rising, "do you want some more to eat?"

"No, no, that's okay," Dorkla replied. "I'm starting to become very sick and tired of having eggs all the time." There was a long pause as they both silently stared at each other with annoyed looks on their faces. Amelia broke through the reverie and carried their dishes over to the dishpan area in the kitchen.

Upon returning to the table, Amelia caught a glimpse of Dorkla's gleaming brown hair and started to notice that it was getting long. Deciding that her hair needed trimming, Amelia turned and headed to the knife rack. After choosing a heavy, rather-sharp one, she brought the knife to the table and commented, "Oh my goodness – your hair – it's way too long."

"But I like it this way Mother," Dorkla protested.

"I really don't give a care," Amelia replied firmly. "It will have to go. You should just be lucky I don't plan on cutting you bald!"

Dorkla looked at her mother angrily. "You wouldn't ever dare to do that to me. I might just run away!" she stated in a threatening tone.

Amelia pushed her down in the chair, grabbed a handful of her long brown hair and began hacking away at it with the knife. "Owww, that hurts!" Dorkla wailed, squirming in her discomfort

"Will you just hold still?" Amelia stated in an exasperated tone of voice. Working her way around Dorkla's small head, she was able to slowly continue trimming her daughter's hair. Brown tresses cascaded to the floor as she worked, but Amelia decided she would clean them up later.

After she was finished with the hair trim, Dorkla was also becoming covered in cut hair strands, so Amelia decided she was definitely in need of a bath to get cleaned up. Dorkla was reluctant to take one, but Amelia grabbed her and dragged her into the room where the big stone tub stood. After heating up water and pouring it into the tub, Amelia handed Dorkla some scented soap and a washcloth. She then pulled off Dorkla's stockings and shoes, then left the room to allow Dorkla some privacy to remove the rest of her clothing and climb into the tub.

Though the oaken door was heavy, Amelia could hear Dorkla exclaiming, "Brrrr!" and "The water's way too cold, Mother! What if I get sick?"

"You'll live, so just deal with it!" Amelia called back to her. She strode down the hallway and settled herself onto a chair in her bedroom. Reaching for a small, leather-bound book and picking up a quill pen, she began writing in her diary. Concentrating on what she wanted to express was made more difficult by the noises Dorkla was making while splashing around in the tub.

Sighing, Amelia tried to give her full attention to her entry and wrote:

"Dear Diary,

I know that I have always been trying to bury a filthy past of sins. I can't possibly be able to change the things I've done. And even though I know that Dorkla's birthday party is tomorrow, I'm not sure if I should tell her or not. Then again, maybe she already knows. Ha, but I doubt it. The pathetic young child's just plain ignorant anyway. There have been many secrets that I've talked about in past entries that seem to still haunt me to this very day. Is it the devil in the details, I wonder? Maybe only God knows. I guess sometimes I'm starting to think that just maybe, Dorkla's words and phrases must be getting into my head and bothering me. I really do care about my dear Dorkla, don't get me wrong, but she's always getting on my nerves because she's always backtalking me. It seems that time and time again, I have to constantly put up with that bastard child. But I guess I would have to blame myself also. I did raise her, didn't I? Is it really Dorkla's fault, or is it just maybe that she really did need a father? It couldn't hurt to have a father figure to possibly be there for her. But I really doubt it because I take very good care of her by myself. Though I must say, these four castle walls have made me long for company. But who really needs friends or a husband for that matter, anyway? It seems Dorkla's all I have, but maybe that's exactly what makes me so sad....."

It was at this time that Amelia had to stop writing in her diary, as Dorkla interrupted her reverie by walking into her mother's room naked. Amelia saw that she was dripping wet from head to toe, soap and water cascading down and onto the stone floor. Dorkla announced in a loud voice, "Mother, I can't seem to find a towel to dry myself."

"Come here," instructed Amelia, waving her to approach with her right hand. Dorkla slowly stepped closer to her mother, shivering in the cold air. Once in front of her mother, Amelia instructed her to turn around, and Dorkla did so. Amelia then reached out and slapped Dorkla's bare buttock with her hand, leaving a red mark in the process.

Dorkla let out a yelp of pained surprise as she was pushed forward, and she began to cry. "Now get in there and put your clothes on." Amelia snapped. "You're mostly dry now, anyway." She wasn't really offended by her daughter not wearing any clothes, Amelia thought to herself. I mean, Jesus had no clothes when he was on the cross, plus Adam and Eve were naked in the Garden of Eden. But I can't have Dorkla running around naked as a jaybird. Besides, what if we end up having some visitors over? I'd be embarrassed to death. Sighing, Amelia decided to just close her diary for the time being.

Setting her quill pen and her diary on the small table in her room, Amelia rose from her chair and made her way back into the kitchen. She found a small slab of beef, which was a rare commodity in Amelia's home. Before long, the delicious smell of the meat cooking wafted through the home, making it easier for Dorkla to want to cheer up and don some clean clothes.

After a short time, Dorkla, now fully clad in silk-stitched nightgown, ran into the kitchen and asked, "What are you cooking, Mother?"

"It's called beef, honey. You've had it before," Amelia responded. "I thought I'd make you feel better by making you something I don't normally make."

Chapter Seven

Dinnertime

Dorkla took her place on one of the chairs at the table and asked, "Mother, when I go to bed tonight, can you please read me a bedtime story?"

"Well, I'll try to see what I can make up for you," Amelia answered.

"What are you talking about?" Dorkla inquired in a puzzled tone. "You mean that you just make up stories that are even real? That makes me wonder if The Bible is made up," she added, sighing deeply.

"Well, how could you really know when you haven't even read it?" Amelia asked, turning her head to look at her daughter.

"That's because you don't let me," Dorkla replied in a surly tone. "The only reason I know about The Bible is because I always hear you talk about it so much, Mother." Amelia didn't answer her, as her attention was turned back towards preparing their meal.

Once the beef and potatoes were cooked thoroughly – a little too done for the meat, Amelia thought to herself with an inward sigh – she placed the platter on the table. As she sat down with her daughter, she could swear she smelled something very familiar – a fragrance that smelled nothing like the scented soap or even the hot food.

Peering over at Dorkla, she asked, anger rising in her tone, "Dorkla, did you put on Mother's perfume again? You already know I told you to stay out of it!"

In a somewhat sad voice, her throat tightening, Dorkla answered, "But Mother, I was just trying to make you happy. You know, I wouldn't try to make you mad on purpose, and besides, don't I smell pretty, Mother?" she asked hopefully. "Plus how am I going to get a suitor if I don't smell good?"

"You know you're way too young to have a suitor," Amelia snapped. "If only just smell attracted men, then I'd have them lining up to greet me at the castle drawbridge, but it does help, though. So how can I stay mad at you?" Amelia smiled at her. "Just make sure you stay out of my make-up."

"Don't you mean castle door, Mother?" Dorkla asked with a grin.

"Ah, there you go again, trying to correct me, Miss Know-It-All," Amelia retorted. "Now just finish eating and shut your trap."

Chapter Eight

Storytime

They both fell silent and began digging into their food. Neither one spoke for the rest of the mealtime. Dorkla's face wore a smirk, but much disappointment mixed with anger and resentment played across Amelia's countenance. As nighttime was upon them once the meal was done, Dorkla headed upstairs to her bedroom, followed by Amelia. She climbed into her large bed, and as Amelia tucked her in, she looked up at her mother. In a small voice she asked, "Are you still mad at me?"

Amelia looked down at her small daughter. "Sort of. I mean kind of. Not really," she replied.

"Okay," Dorkla answered in a relieved tone. "Will you please read me a story like you said you would?" she asked anxiously.

"I guess so," Amelia replied in an offhand way, "if it really makes you happy. I guess you don't forget about anything, do you? But remember, you know, I'm not very good with stories."

"Well, that's all right," Dorkla said persistently. "Just try and give it your best shot."

Amelia then seated herself on the edge of Dorkla's bed and began. "All right, let's see here. Once upon a time, there lived some people in someplace. They kissed some frog, became princes and princesses and lived happily after. The end." She stood up, turned around and bent over her daughter. "Now goodnight and try to get some sleep." She kissed Dorkla on the forehead, then strode out of the room and headed downstairs.

"That's it??" Dorkla shouted after her in disbelief. "What kind of a story was that? I must be the frog or something." Amelia ignored her daughter's comments as she continued down the stairs, pausing at a window to gaze out at the fog. Although it didn't appear to be as thick as what it was last night, it was still a somewhat soothing, mystifying experience to behold.

The water in the moat sparkled in the moonlight that could penetrate the fog and settle on the landscape as Dorkla held her pillow tightly in her arms, which in some ways brought a little comfort to her. She was very lonely, due in no small part to not having any friends. She would get lost in a dream of playing outside, getting the chance to play make-believe and just having someone besides her mother to talk to. Also, Dorkla hated the feeling of never really having someone with whom to share things. It wasn't that she couldn't ever related to her stupid mother. There were times when she definitely could, but she was scarcely able to relate to the nastiness her mother conceived. That was something difficult for Dorkla to handle, but she tried not to let her mother get the best of her.

On the other hand, Amelia's dreams were very pleasant. Her nighttime thoughts were filled with images of many gold and silver coins ready to spend and thinking of a castle with absolutely no Dorkla to be seen or found. This way of thinking is why many mothers and daughters simply don't seem to get along sometimes. They somehow have different ideas of where they should belong in life.

The hours passed along through the night to reveal a completely new but same old everyday sunrise. Dorkla was the very first to wake up again, as she always did. A few minutes later, her mother awakened and stepped into the kitchen, yawning and stretching as she made her way down the hallway.

Dorkla was so excited, as today was her birthday. She was in a very good mood, but not about having to eat more eggs. Ahh yuck, she thought to herself, expecting the worst, but she was very relieved to see muffins and other quickbreads along with fruit juice, a few rare oranges, yeast bread and a crock of jelly instead of eggs for once.

Amelia turned and smiled at her daughter. "Are you planning on having a good day today, a day filled with fun and celebration?" she asked.

Dorkla answered in a sarcastic tone, "Yes, Mother. I already know I'm having a birthday party."

Chapter Nine

The Big Day

Amelia looked at her daughter angrily. "How dare you? Don't you get mouthy with me, you Dorkla! It's still very early in the morning. You should know that I was in a good mood until you ruined it."

Dorkla responded, "Yeah, whatever, Mother." They both laughed over the silliness of what they just said and decided to just let it go and not let it bother them.

After a hearty breakfast, they got dressed and headed into Kodaya City, essentially to buy Dorkla her birthday presents, a dress and a birthday cake from the baker's. As they walked towards the city, Dorkla looked up and noticed that it was starting to get cloudy. She felt a breeze begin to kick up and felt it blowing her shorn locks around. As always, rather than walk alongside her mother, Dorkla followed her.

Lately, it seemed that no one talked about or yelled about Queen Amelia, treating her like some sort of royalty or important person anymore. It seemed, though, that deep down she was craving their attention more now than ever before. The charm of her being a queen had worn off by now. Amelia wished just to shrug it off as if it didn't bother her.

At the baker's, they looked at all of their choices and decided on a chocolate cake with white frosting all over, strawberry frosting for trim and real strawberries laid in a circular pattern along the top, as this was the favorite for both of them. Amelia took a few silver coins out of her coin bag and handed them to the baker. He carefully set the cake in a wooden box so that she could get it back to the castle safely.

They left the baker's and went straight for the shop where Dorkla had espied her pretty red dress. Amelia handed the shopkeeper a gold coin and a few silver ones. Once the transaction was completed, he carefully wrapped the dress up in a parcel to help keep it from wrinkling and fastened it with string, then handed it to Amelia. She took it from him, turned away, then turned back to face him. "Do you know who I am?" she asked him.

The shopkeeper looked a little uncomfortable as he stammered, "You're, um – that queen, aren't you?"

Amelia looked annoyed. "Well, it sure took you long enough to say it! I guess it seems my people are starting to forget about who I am. Well, they'd better not, or I might just start raising taxes again!" She turned on her heel and stormed out of the store, Dorkla running after her to try to keep up.

Her face dark with anger, Amelia strode purposefully back to the castle, holding tightly to the cake and the parcel containing Dorkla's new dress. Once back inside, Amelia was getting even angrier, as they discovered that someone had been in the castle while they were gone to the city. A few things were smashed on the floor, and other things were thrown hither and about. What they were looking for, Amelia and Dorkla weren't exactly sure, but they definitely wouldn't let this happen again if Amelia had her say in it. Amelia turned to her daughter and asked, "Dorkla, did you happen to bolt the door before we left?"

Dorkla replied naively, "No, I didn't. I thought you were supposed to have done that. Oh, and I accidentally left the door open."

"Good going, numbskull!" Amelia retorted. "It seems possible that your dimwitted actions could have gotten us robbed big-time. You're lucky that I don't ground you to the castle for life!"

"But I didn't mean it, honest!" Dorkla pleaded in a whiny, irritating voice.

"All right. Let's just forget about it," Amelia replied in a weary tone. "Just go to your room and try on your new dress for Mother, okay my darling?"

"Oh yes, Mother!" Dorkla exclaimed, relieved to have her mother on another, more cheerful topic. "I'll be back in a flash," she added, seizing the parcel and running towards the stairs to her room. After she left, Amelia saw a pile of clean clothing left on a table and began folding it.

When Dorkla returned to the room, Amelia gasped at the sight of her daughter in the breathtaking new gown. It looked even prettier on Dorkla than it did on the store display. "Oh, Dorkla," she exclaimed, "it most definitely looks beautiful on you, darling!"

Upon hearing her mother's words, Dorkla ran into her mother's arms. Amelia lifted her daughter up and gave her a big hug. With her arms firmly around her mother's neck, Dorkla whispered, "Thank you, Mother. This is the best birthday present I've ever had!"

Amelia set her back down on the floor and stated, "Okay now, that's good. Now go and take the dress back off. You need to go and get changed. That way, you won't get any cake or frosting on it." Dorkla set off for her room to do as she was told.

While Dorkla was attending to her mother's request, Amelia began to prepare the table for their little party. She gingerly set the cake on the table, taking care to not smear any of the frosting. She then found eight small candles, set them into the cake and lit them. Once that was done, she went to the cupboard, got out plates and cups, then went to a drawer and got out two forks. She set out all of that on the table, then filled each cup with a little milk.

After completing her preparations, Amelia wearily sat down in one of the chairs by the table. Just then, Dorkla returned to the room, having changed into a simple cotton frock. Amelia turned in her chair and called, "Oh, Dorkla, I forgot to get the big knife for cutting the cake. Could you please be a dear and go get it for me?"

"Yes, Mother, in just a minute," Dorkla answered obediently. She turned toward the kitchen. It was somewhat difficult for Dorkla to reach the knife rack in the drawer, as she wasn't very tall and the drawer in which the knives were kept was rather deep. But by standing on her tiptoes and reaching as far as she could, she was able to grasp the knife's handle and pull it out of the drawer. Turning, she headed back to the table and Amelia.

However, Dorkla was never taught the proper way to carry a knife, and she still had a firm grip on the handle, with the point facing forward, as she approached her mother. Hearing Dorkla's footsteps nearing, Amelia turned slightly in the chair, saying, "Oh, thank you very much, honey." As she turned, she tried to reach for the knife with her right hand. But something went terribly wrong. Her chair tipped towards her daughter , and as Dorkla watched in horror, the knife plunged into her mother's left side!

Dorkla and Amelia both fell to the ground, with Dorkla still gripping the knife's handle. This can't be happening, Dorkla thought to herself. As Amelia's blood gushed down around the blade, Dorkla shouted, "Ohhh, I'm so sorry, Mother!"

In shock but able to still speak, Amelia replied in a tight voice, "It's all right," trying to reassure her daughter that she wasn't angry at her. With the knife still embedded in Amelia's side, Dorkla pushed her over in an effort to pull it out. With a mighty heave, the knife slowly came back out of its entrance hole; however, once it did, Amelia began to bleed profusely. Gazing down at her wound, Amelia asked, "Dorkla, will you please go and fetch your mother a rag?"

Dorkla absentmindedly responded, "Um, don't you mean a towel, Mother?" trying to correct her mother again at an absolutely worst time.

Amelia groaned in agony. "Whatever! Just go and get it, for crying out loud!" she shouted with as much energy as she could muster. At her words, Dorkla scurried away towards the linen closet and seized a couple towels, remembering at this moment where to find them.

At this most-inopportune time, there was a loud knock on the heavy castle door. This struck Dorkla as odd, for to her knowledge, they had no friends or known living relatives. However, she was in need of someone to help her mother, so she realized she had little choice but to see who was there. Returning to her mother's side, she bent down and gently placed the towels on her mother's wound. Amelia, in spite of her pain, managed to wrap them around to form a makeshift bandage from them.

Rising from her mother, Dorkla ran for the door, and pulling with all of her small weight, managed to pull it open. Standing in front of her was a man about Amelia's age. He was clean-shaven, and his brown hair was neatly trimmed as well. Although she was curious as to whom he might be, finding out that information didn't seem important at the moment because there wasn't any time. Her main concern was to try to stop her mother from bleeding anymore. There would be time to get acquainted later; however, she was glad to have some company for once. Looking up at him with tears in her eyes, she stammered, "Oh....um.... please come in, um, whoever you are." Dorkla seized his hand and pulled in him in to see her mother, who was slowly dying.

Chapter Ten

The Visitor

The stranger took one look at the situation and made a sound of disgust. "Oh, great. What's wrong with her? What did you do?"

"Uh, what do you mean?" Dorkla asked in a defensive tone. "Why do you think it's my fault?" Why do children always get the blame when something goes wrong, she asked herself.

"It doesn't matter what I think. That's not at all important anyway. But I need you to help me lift and carry her to her bed," the visitor responded in a less-accusatory manner as he gestured toward Amelia with both hands.

"But why?" Dorkla inquired.

The visitor looked at her with annoyance. "What do you think? Because I don't want her to bleed to death." Looking sternly at Dorkla, the thought crossed his mind that this is a stubborn child, something she got from her mother.

Dorkla looked at him in dismay. "What? You'd rather she bleed on her bed? I thought you were going to help save her life!" she exclaimed, disappointment evident in her tone.

The stranger looked at her patiently. "That's what I'm going to do. I'm planning on helping her, but right now I need your help, Dorkla," he said, his voice rising as he spoke.

Dorkla was even more puzzled than before. "But...but....how do you know my name? Who exactly are you? I don't even know who *you* are!" she stated, astonished.

The visitor didn't answer her question. "I must say that I'm sorry I don't have any time as of now to tell you," he said in a gentle tone. "Let's just say there's a lot you don't know about me."

Finding it pointless to push for information at this time, Dorkla fell silent and bent to the task of assisting the stranger in lifting and moving her mother out of the kitchen. However, her mind was whirling by what he meant by his last statement. Bringing her out of her reverie, he instructed her to get on one side as he got on the other, then they both crouched and gently picked Amelia up off the floor. She groaned in pain as they did so, even though they tried to be careful, but they gingerly carried her to her bed and made her as comfortable as they could.

Looking down, they discovered that they both had blood on their hands and clothes. Retracing their steps, they found a small trail of blood spots and a large puddle where Amelia had fallen. The knife, its handle and blade also covered in blood, still lay on the floor where Dorkla had dropped it once she'd removed it from her mother.

Stepping over to the kitchen water pump, Dorkla got the water running and washed off her hands. Glancing back over her shoulder, Dorkla noticed that the visitor didn't go to the trouble; he just wiped his hands on his pants, which were already dirty, it looked, by the paint stains on them. Once her hands were clean, she turned and looked at the mess. I should really get this cleaned up, she thought to herself. But I can do that later.

Out of the corner of her eye, she saw that the visitor was almost to the castle door. His hand was reaching for the door latch when Dorkla shouted, "Mister, where are you going? Please come back. Weren't you going to still help my mother?" Her eyes were pleading as well as her voice.

The visitor looked down at her and in a kindly tone, stated, "Don't you know that I already did? My help here really is no longer needed. So just let me leave already."

Dorkla took hold of his forearm. "Oh, no," she begged. "Please don't go. My mother might still need your help. Could you stay for awhile? We can have some egg sandwiches or steak, depending on what food my mother has left. And I haven't figured out yet who you even are. If you do leave now, I might never find out."

The visitor pulled away from her grasp but didn't step away. "I really need to get going, but I guess if it suits you, I could stay for maybe a little longer. Besides, your mother will be all right. She just needs to get some rest." Looking down at her and sighing, the visitor added, "Oh fine. I guess I should finally tell you who I am or why I know who you are." He turned around, walked back into the kitchen and sat down on a chair.

Dorkla peered at him intently. "Okay, then, who are you?" she said after a long pause.

The visitor took a deep breath. "All right, enough already," he began. "I'll tell you. You won't believe me, but I am, well, used to be, King Davia. Well, now it's just Davia."

Dorkla sat down suddenly in a chair in astonishment. "You're right. I don't believe you!" she blurted out.

"Well, what do you mean?" Davia asked. It was now his turn to be puzzled. "Why is that?"

"Because you're dead," Dorkla stated flatly. "I mean, he's dead. That is, that's what my mother told me." She suddenly found it very difficult to take a breath.

Davia stared at her in surprise for a long minute. Then he said, "Well, I'm not even close to kicking the bucket. From the likes of it, I'm alive and well. You can see me right now!"

Dorkla looked very thoughtful. Then her face brightened as she said, "So you... you're my father than."

Davia smiled at her. "You've guessed it! Seems nothing gets by you. Sure took you a long time to figure that out." He looked closely at her. "My, have you grown!" he said, enthusiasm in his voice.

Dorkla jumped up from her chair, ran around the table to Davia, and gave him a big hug. "Oh, Father, you're really home!" she cried. "I missed you so much!"

"How could you possibly remember knowing me?" Davia asked. "It was so long ago. We didn't really get to see each other." He stopped, not sure if he should tell her more.

"How come?" she asked, returning to her chair.

Davia put his hands on the table, then said, "Go get me something to drink, please, and then I'll tell you."

Dorkla pushed one of the already-poured milk cups over to Davia. "You can have it. My birthday's ruined anyway," she said in a sad tone. "But as you were saying," she prodded.

Davia took a long drink from the cup, then began his story. "I was born in a little village. Went to school for awhile, then ever since. My parents sold me in to slavery. One day after working for someone else for years, your mother bought me. Forced me to make a baby with her, which explains how you were born. I worked outside sometimes tending the fields and local castle gardens plus other household chores. She would always keep a close eye on me to make sure that I didn't ever run away. Then one day she decided that she didn't have any need for me anymore. She brought me to the market in Kodaya and found a buyer. Then she sold me for, get this, a couple measly few coins. I'm for sure worth more than that! I mean, come on, seriously."

"So did you and my mother get married before you had me?" Dorkla inquired.

Davia looked at her patiently. "Like I just told you, she forced me to be with her. I would have really liked to have been married though in a church and have a wedding cake."

Chapter Eleven

Fourteen Characteristics of a Serial Killer

" Speaking of cake," he added, "can I have some of your birthday cake?"

"Yes, go ahead," Dorkla replied, sighing. "Why don't you just eat the whole thing? Who cares? As I said, my birthday's over with, thanks to my mess-up."

Davia looked at her curiously. "Are you saying Amelia's accident was partly your fault?"

Dorkla looked despondent. "It's really more, completely my fault," she said sadly. "I didn't mean to do it. I went to fetch my mother a knife and came back. When I was behind her with it, she fell backwards onto it." Tears came to her eyes as she spoke.

"You should very well know that I believe you," Davia said gently. "To tell you the truth, I'm not very fond of her your mother anyway. From the way she treated me, I would have stabbed her in the back the first chance I got." His voice became bitter as he spoke.

"But that's all in the past, right?" Dorkla asked hopefully. "She might have changed since you last knew her."

Davia didn't answer her. Instead, he dug his hands into the cake, grabbing a hunk of it which he began stuffing into his mouth. Once done, he got up, found a bucket and a clean rag and swabbed all the blood off of the floor. Finally, he said, "Changed, unlikely. I highly doubt it," as he bent down to pick up the knife still on the floor.

Dorkla finally gave in to the sweet smell of the cake and got herself a piece, which tasted pretty good, especially considering it was the first thing she'd had to eat in hours. By that time, it was getting dark. Once she'd had her fill of cake, she realized that even though she was officially a year older, she didn't really feel it.

Although by that time it was her usual bedtime, she wasn't told that she had to go to sleep, as her mother was completely out of it from losing so much blood. But having been kept to a strict schedule for so many years, Dorkla was used to going to bed at the same time every night. Rubbing her eyes and yawning, she was becoming sleepy.

Before she went to bed, she told Davia that he could use the guest room to sleep. Davia decided he would stay for tonight, but he was unsure as to whether he wanted to even sleep in a castle that brought back bad memories of his past.

During the night, a thunderstorm rolled in, awakening both Dorkla and Davia. They got up and covered the windows to help keep the rain from coming in, then went back to sleep, which came easily to Dorkla. She enjoyed the sounds of rain and the thunder, as it soothed and comforted her; it didn't frighten her as it did some children, and after she fell asleep, the storm dissipated.

When Dorkla woke up in the morning, she pulled back the curtains to reveal a magnificent rainbow in the sky. It occurred to her the thought about the rainbow that appeared after the Great Flood in Noah's day. Dorkla pondered that the rainbow must appear after it rains so that people wouldn't panic every time it rains, thinking that there would be another Great Flood again like God promised.

Dorkla made her way downstairs to find Davia finishing preparing breakfast for them. She saw scrambled eggs and fruit juice on the table. Glancing around the kitchen,

Davia commented, "You're right. Your mother sure has a lot of eggs and not much else. Doesn't she ever go shopping for food?

Dorkla shook her head. "No, we don't get out much," she replied. "So where's Amelia?"

"Who's that?" Davia asked jokingly.

"Um, my mother, stupid," answered Dorkla, slightly annoyed. "So where's she at? She should have been in here by now. Also, I must ask you – were you here yesterday when we were gone to the city? Because when we got back, the whole place was a mess. I think it still is. Oops, I mean was," she added, looking around.

Davia looked puzzled. "No, I wasn't here. Honestly. But I did clean this place up earlier this morning," he replied.

Dorkla picked up a forkful of eggs and waved them around. "You're Davia, my father. Right?"

Chapter Twelve

Ashes to Ashes, Dust to Dust

"Then why did my mother tell a fib and say you were dead?" Dorkla asked.

Heaving a great sigh, Davia replied, "I seriously don't know, so let's go ask her in person, shall we?" They finished the rest of their meal in silence.

Once done, Davia pushed himself away from the table and brought their plates to the counter to be washed later. The two of them left the kitchen and headed towards Amelia's room. "All right, okay then. But I hope she's not sleeping. She gets mad when you awaken her when she wants to sleep in."

As they stepped into Amelia's bedroom, they couldn't tell if she was still conscious or even if she was still bleeding. Dorkla went over to her mother and gently nudged her with both hands, saying, "Mother, wake up."

Davia then put his hand above Amelia's nose to check to see if she was still breathing. Unfortunately, no breath could be felt or found. He then checked her pulse by putting his finger on her neck and wrist. He felt badly, as he knew there wasn't a heartbeat in her body, only that she was ice-cold. It was apparent that Amelia was dead and gone, and Dorkla had to deal with this shock. Davia, in spite of what Amelia had done to him in the past, felt sympathy, not only for Amelia but for his little daughter and her loss.

As realization came over her features, Dorkla got very wide-eyed and began to shout, "Oh, no, Mother, don't! Don't go, please! I can't carry on without you!" She collapsed on the side of the bed next to Amelia. Crying, moaning and whining, Dorkla gasped out, "It's.... it's all my fault. I killed her. I'm a murderer."

Davia suddenly knelt and gathered Dorkla up in his strong arms, saying in a soothing tone, "No, don't say that. How could you think that way? Your mother wouldn't have wanted you to live your life consumed with remorse. You should have already known that. It was an accident; you told me yourself."

Dorkla pushed herself free of her father's grasp without a word and ran to her bedroom to hide. Davia sighed and began debating what he should do. Not in terms of attending to Dorkla's emotional needs, but what to do with Amelia's dead body, a corpse that would soon begin rotting.

As he looked around her room, he saw a quill pen loosely clasped in Amelia's hand, signifying that she had previously been writing something down before she grew too weak and passed away. A first glance failed to find any papers she had been writing on, but a more-thorough search revealed her diary lying open on the table next to the bed.

"Dorkla, could you please come back in here?" he called out to her. "Quickly, I found something you need to see!" However, figuring that she was too griefstricken to return to Amelia's room at this point, he dashed out of Amelia's bedroom and took the stairs two at a time to Dorkla's bedroom.

Upon reaching Dorkla's room, he discovered her curled up next to her bed, her shoulders heaving from the force of her sobs. Davia touched her gently. "Dorkla, I know that your mother's dead. I can't help that now. But I have some good news. So I need you to listen to me."

Dorkla cocked her head up and looked at her father through tear-flooded eyes. "Go away!" she demanded. "Just leave me alone right now! I don't give a care, you hear me?" She put her head back down upon her knees and resumed sobbing.

Davia looked at his daughter sympathetically but knew that she needed to hear what he had to say. He took hold of her left arm and said, "I know you're hurting, but you *will* listen to me. For one thing, I've had it up to here with your attitude. I can't stand it any more. Why, Dorkla, does it seem that you have to be so complicated? I guess your mother didn't raise you right, did she?"

Davia's last statement got Dorkla's attention. Her face grew red with anger as she shouted, "Don't you dare talk about my mother like that! I've known her a lot longer than you ever did. I was there for her when she cried, when she laughed!"

Davia cut her rantings off. "Or when she yelled at you and argued? Don't think I don't know. I lived with her at one time, too. I knew the way she was!"

Dorkla looked at him defiantly. "Well, that's beside the point. Anyway, she was my mother. And, and, I loved her very much, but you didn't know that, did you?"

Davia bent down and looked directly into her eyes. "You should know I also loved your mother. Despite the way she acted. Why do you think I came back?"

"So you could see me," Dorkla responded.

Davia laughed a little. "That, too," he answered.

Hearing her father say that cheered Dorkla up. She rose off the floor and gave Davia a hug, but not as big a one as she'd given him earlier, but he was grateful to receive it.

Setting her on his lap, Davia continued. "Now about your mom. She left a message to you before she died."

Dorkla looked amazed. "How could she get the strength to write me something when she was slowly dying?"

"I'm not sure exactly," Davia answered thoughtfully, "but you should definitely read it."

The main reason that Dorkla was taking her mother's death so hard was because up until now, no one in her life had ever died. Since she mostly lived alone with her mother, Amelia would sometimes talk about death with her, always trying to convince her that her father was deceased. But until she actually experienced it so close to her, it just didn't register as real.

Dorkla dashed out of her room and down the stairs to Amelia's bedroom. She grabbed for Amelia's diary and scanned it from top to bottom. Dorkla knew that this was the very book her mother always told her to step away from and yelled at her many times for even touching it. One time she picked it up and held it, but Amelia came into the room and slapped it out of her hands. Why would she even want to write something to her, she wasn't at all sure. None of that mattered anymore since she was gone. She couldn't tell her what to do ever again.

Dorkla sat down in a chair, opened the diary and began reading. This was something she had learned from her mother, as she was read so many bedtime story books. She also taught herself, was able to memorize the alphabet and count on her fingers to learn numbers.

Chapter Thirteen

Amelia's Last Words

She had a hard time, though, spelling out the big words. Dorkla held her hands still on the last entry Amelia wrote as she began to read:

"Dear Diary,

I'm aware that this may be the last entry I will ever write. So Lord, I ask forgiveness and confess all of my many sins. May my soul find peace as I rest. Dorkla, don't blame yourself. I'm going to leave this Earth someday anyway, and I probably deserve to for the misery, I'm sure, I put you through. Know that you are special, and I love you."

At this point, Dorkla had to stop reading for a few minutes and swab at the tears that were streaming down her face. Once her vision cleared and she had regained her composure, she continued reading:

"You are the child I always wanted, and nothing ever can change that. King Davia, please take care of her."

At reading these words, Dorkla almost laughed out loud at the thought that her mother still considered calling Davia a king. She continued on:

"It appears that I am now growing weary, so I must soon stop writing. So I must be brief. If......"

Dorkla looked in dismay at her mother's final few words, wishing there was more, like her mother telling them good-bye. Dorkla sat there in silence and puzzlement. "What did she mean? If what?" she asked herself as she closed the diary.

Davia's words broke through her reverie. "Does it really even matter?" She looked up to see him standing in the doorway.

I guess not, Dorkla thought to herself.

Davia moved closer to Dorkla and added, "That leaves us with only one thing left to do."

Dorkla jerked her head up to look at her father. "What's that?" she asked in a polite tone.

Davia gently sighed. "What do you think? We need to get rid of your mother's body, especially before it starts decomposing." Dorkla looked at him and frowned; however, she knew it had to be done.

They positioned themselves, as they did before, on either side of her now-cold body. She seemed a bit heavier now that she was dead, Dorkla thought to herself. As they gently carried her out of her room, huffing and puffing at the effort, Davia glanced up at Dorkla and asked, "So where do you possibly think that we could bring her to be buried? Do you have any ideas?"

Dorkla found it difficult to keep her balance as she was holding onto her mother's body, but she managed to gasp out, "Out back. There's a place where my mother said that you were buried." They made their way out of the castle and headed around back to the location Dorkla had described. Once they got out into the cool air, though, Amelia's body seemed to begin stiffening with rigor mortis. Dorkla noticed that the air was still damp from the recent rain, but unfortunately so was the ground, so it was a little difficult for them to carry her as the pathway had gotten rather muddy. However, with even greater effort and one instance of almost falling down, they finally made their way to the designated spot without either of them slipping or getting too dirty. They carefully set her down next to where she would be buried.

Davia turned to Dorkla. "Please go and get the shovel from the shed."

Chapter Fourteen

R.I.P.

The shed wasn't far away. It only took Dorkla fifteen footsteps to get there. The shed was also created with bricks, like the castle, to try to camouflage it, making it blend in with the rest of the castle. It contained not only a few shovels, but various tools and items that were needed out of doors, such as an assortment of gardening tools, wooden buckets of several different sizes and a few old bags of chicken feed, even though there were no longer any chickens at the castle.

Dorkla pushed open the heavy wooden door and peered inside. As her eyes got accustomed to the gloom, she saw that the shovels were hung on pegs that held up other tools as well. She chose a shovel and pulled it down. It was rather heavy, but she managed to drag it out of the shed by its handle and over to where Davia was waiting. She leaned the handle towards him, saying cheerfully, "Here you go," proud of her small accomplishment. She wasn't happy to be helping bury her mother by any means. She was still very sad inside, but she was glad to lend a hand to her father.

Davia reached for the handle and smiled gently at his daughter. "Thank you very much, Dorkla," he told her. The soil was already wet from the rains and not hard or sun-baked, so digging the hole, although hard work, was made much easier. The shovel bit into the ground near the rock Dorkla had earlier set flowers. Working diligently, he scooped up large piles of dirt, emptying the shovel into a growing pile next to the hole. Davia stopped for only a moment halfway through his task to wipe the sweat from his brow.

He then continued on until he hit a hard surface with his shovel. Puzzled, he freed it from its earthen hiding place and handed it to Dorkla. It was a small wooden box with metal hinges and hasp.

"What's inside this?" she asked, as puzzled as her father. Why would Amelia bury a box? she wondered to herself. Probably to convince Dorkla that Davia was dead in case she had to dig it up But now was not the time to consider it any further.

By this point, Davia had finished digging the gravesite. Dorkla set the box on the ground, and they positioned themselves on both sides of Amelia, lifted her once more and placed her into the hole. They knew that it would be very disrespectful to just kick or push the body into the grave. Davia reached down and positioned her body so as to make it look as nice as he could.

However, before covering it over with soil, both Dorkla and Davia had some last words they wanted to say. Davia set the shovel down and began speaking first. "Amelia, my sweet Amelia. May it be that we should meet again in the next life. Then I'll hold you so deep within my heart as long as I live. Know that you were my hope during the darkest of times. It was you who helped me to carry on. I will honor your request of taking care of Dorkla. So – I guess – until we meet again someday. Good-bye and farewell." Davia stepped back so that Dorkla could have her turn.

She bowed her head as she began, "Mother, could it be that you're there? Is it true that you are possibly listening? Thank you for just being there for me. I really miss you now and always will. It sure hurts and becomes very painful to have to admit that I was sometimes a handful. I know that I was a problem child who most often got in the way. I wish you could forgive me for all the many times I was bad. Did I tell you yet how much that I still love you? Well, I'll wait for you if you continue to wait for me in Heaven. I certainly hope you will." There was a moment of silence as her words drifted off in the wind. After giving her a respectful time for quiet contemplation, Davia picked the shovel back up and began pushing soil into the grave around and on Amelia's body. Once all the grave was completely covered up, they stood there for another moment, then made their way back to the shed and the castle, with Dorkla awkwardly carrying the wooden box.

Chapter Fifteen

Bad Dreams

Once they reached the castle's interior, Dorkla set the heavy box on the table. Davia offered to prepare the noon meal for Dorkla, but she looked sadly at her father and replied, "No, that's all right. I'm not very hungry right now. I think I'll go lie down for awhile." She turned and headed upstairs to her room to take a nap.

Davia sat down at the table and looked at the box. Although he was curious as to its contents, he decided not to try to open it until after Dorkla awakened from her rest, as it would seem rather rude to check out what it held without her present. He did know that it contained *something*, though, as it made a little rattling noise when Dorkla had set it down.

Upstairs, sleep eluded Dorkla. She was still depressed, full of sorrow and felt horrible inside. She was constantly replaying over and over in her mind the very painful events of what she had done to her mother. Echoes of the past hours still haunted her even as she finally drifted off to sleep.

Dorkla's dreams were so vivid that her body twitched restlessly as she slept. When she dreamed, her dreams were about Amelia still being alive, well and living in the castle. Amelia was telling Dorkla what to do, much as she did when she was alive. Dorkla dreamt that Amelia was sitting very watchfully at the table as she asked, "What are you doing, Dorkla? Will you get in here already?" Dorkla was in her room. She was sitting and playing with some toys. Dorkla, in her sleep stage, knew this had to be a dream because she didn't own very many toys in real life. All she actually owned was a raggedy old doll that was missing an eye and had some of the cotton stuffing missing due to a small hole torn in it. It was one of the few gifts Dorkla had even received from her mother.

Dorkla answered her mother, "I'm a…. I'm just playing, Mother! I'm not doing anything wrong."

Amelia demanded, "Well, didn't you hear me? Come here now!"

"Okay, okay, Mother. I'll be right there in a minute," Dorkla called, filled with great fear that her mother was very mad at her for some reason.

"I don't know – how about this second?" Amelia called back.

Strolling into the room, Dorkla was hesitating when it came to seeing her mother's reaction to disobeying. She decided to remain obedient by pleasing and honoring her requests. However, her good intentions faded with her mother's harsh tone. "You really should know that I am getting sick of you being mouthy and refusing to even listsen to me. When I tell you to do something, I want you to do it the first time I tell you, not the last!" Amelia spat out.

Strange as it may have seemed, even in her dreams they still argued. Dorkla forced herself to answer in a humble tone. "Yes, Mother, I understand," she answered meekly.

Amelia stood up and placed her left hand gently on Dorkla's right shoulder. "Dorkla, I have something important to ask you," she stated in an urgent tone. At these words, Amelia placed her right hand on Dorkla's left shoulder so she could have her daughter facing her directly.

"What? What is it, Mother?" Dorkla asked, as her body began to tremble.

Amelia moved her hands to encircle Dorkla's neck and began choking her, shouting, "Why, Dorkla? Why did you kill me? What did I ever do to you?"

Dorkla woke up gasping for breath and then screaming, realizing that her own hands were around her neck. As she became aware of her surroundings, she was very saddened. This wasn't the way she wanted to remember her mother or to have a dream of her, either.

Davia rushed into the room, hastening to reassure her. "Quiet! Calm down, Dorkla! All you had was just a frightening nightmare," he stated in a gentle voice as he took hold of her wrists.

"Oh, it's worse than that!" Dorkla cried out, trying to catch her breath.

"Well, it's all right," Davia spoke in a soothing tone. "You're going to be okay." He gently rubbed her wrists with his fingers, then let them go.

Dorkla sat upright, still trembling. "It was so awful!" she told her father. "I don't think that my mother has forgiven me at all. In my dream, she wanted to kill me and take revenge!"

Davia looked lovingly at his pale, shaken daughter and replied "Don't you know that you need to realize, Dorkla, that it was just that, a dream and nothing more. I know that with your mother now dead, you seem to have trouble trying to just let go."

Dorkla kicked back her covers and turned so that her feet were touching the floor, then answered, "Yes, I know, but...."

"But what?" Davia wanted to know.

"What if it's true? What if she's mad at me still? Dreams do convey realities sometimes, don't they? Maybe she's going to come back from the dead and haunt me in a ghost form!" she said, still badly frightened.

"Don't be silly," her father retorted. "You're being ridiculous. Dreams are just illusions in your head when you sleep, nothing more, okay? Besides, ghosts don't exist!"

"That may be," Dorkla replied, "but I still think the dream might mean something. That makes me scared to even go back to sleep."

Chapter Sixteen

What's In the Box?

Davia smiled at his daughter. "You'll be fine! Now let's go into the kitchen and have some of what I've prepared." He stood up and headed toward her bedroom door.

"Well, I guess so," Dorkla admitted. "So what did you make?"

"Something that's completely different than what you've had before," he answered cheerfully.

Dorkla realized that her stomach *was* rumbling from not having eaten anything in a long while. "Sounds good!" she mustered, feeling a little better. "I hope it's not eggs again for the thousandth time."

"We're having oatmeal mush, actually," Davia replied.

Dorkla looked surprised. "Oatmeal? Where did you get that? From what I remember, my mother hadn't purchased any of that since I last checked."

"I found some in the shed where you got the shovel. I noticed it in the back corner when I went to put the shovel back in its proper place." They both left Dorkla's room and went down the stairs to the kitchen. The box was still on the table where Dorkla had left it. She stared at it with wide eyes as she pulled her chair out and sat down, wondering what its contents may be.

Davia went to the fireplace. Using a pot hook, he hefted a pot of steaming oatmeal away from the fire and onto the table. He grasped a ladle and scooped some out into a bowl and handed it to Dorkla. He then ladled out some for himself as well, cautioning Dorkla to take care as to not burn herself. Davia fetched a pitcher containing milk and poured some into two cups for Dorkla and himself. Then he sat down at his place, ready to eat his food, but looked over at his daughter. "I know that it seems exceedingly difficult to eat at a time like this, now that Amelia is dead and all," he said gently.

Dorkla leaned over her bowl, feeling the steam of the oatmeal warm up her face. She then looked up at her father. "Pardon me, but I'd much rather not have a conversation about her right now," she replied flatly.

"I understand what you mean," Davia answered thoughtfully. "Like I said, it's hard to talk about. But please, at least don't shut me out. I'm always here for you."

"What are you saying?" Dorkla demanded. "You're always here for me, you sure have not been! So where were you precisely after all these years? I was even led to believe that you were dead! That is, until recently." Her eyes filled with angry tears.

Davia looked impatient. "First of all," he stated, his voice rising, "I already told you before, didn't I, Dorkla? You know I was a slave for all those years. Second, it wasn't at all humanly possible for me to do anything within my reach to visit you. I'd have been whipped for sure had I tried."

Dorkla was abashed. "I guess if you put it that way," she answered in a humble tone, "then I forgive you, Father. I remember what you told me. I think I was just trying to see if you cared."

Davia glanced down at her bowl. "I see that your oatmeal has cooled down by now," he stated, changing the subject.

She looked down at his bowl. "I think so has yours," she answered with a giggle, putting her hand up to her mouth. They both fell silent as they commenced eating their food. Once done, Davia picked up their dishes and began cleaning up after the meal, while Dorkla felt it was definitely time to see what was in the box.

She moved the metal hasp over to the side, wiping off some dirt as she did so. With a little jiggling, she was able to maneuver the lid and open it. Peering over the edge and into the box, the first thing she saw was leaves. Old, dry leaves. Digging deeper, though, she saw there was more. At the bottom she found chicken bones. Why? She wondered. Maybe Amelia was wanting to fake Davia's death just in case Dorkla wanted to see his remains.

There was one bone in particular that caught her attention because wrapped around it was a bronze ring. It didn't seem very special at first to Dorkla. She called Davia over to look at it. "What is this, Father?" she inquired.

Davia looked at it, thoughtfully turning it over in his hands. "It looks familiar, actually," he answered after a long pause. "I remember someone in a village giving it to Amelia to pay for their taxes."

"So it's just a ring?" Dorkla asked, disappointment in her voice. "How boring is that? So, who was the person who gave it? Do you still possibly remember who it was?"

"Yes," answered Davia. "He should still be alive and living in the Cilowick Village. His name is Dr. Sarnic. We can go visit him now, if you'd like. It's not that far. It's right past Kodaya."

"Sure, but we have to hurry so that we can get back before it gets dark," Dorkla replied. "He's a doctor, but why is he living in a village? I thought doctors made lots of money. I didn't know boys wore rings," she added naively.

"Well, they don't make that much money when someone else charges such high taxes," Davia retorted. "And the ring, he told me, was from his deceased wife."

After donning cloaks, they set off for Cilowick, traveling through Kodaya's main street on the way. They didn't stop to buy anything, but they did stop by a pawn shop to see how much value the ring had. They were both surprised when the pawn shop owner offered them a hundred gold coins for it.

"Wow," said Dorkla gleefully, "Then that means this ring is actually worth a lot and must be more valuable than I thought!"

After leaving the pawn shop, they continued on to Cilowick. Arriving at the village, they realized they could remove their cloaks, as it was getting hot. They found the doctor's address and knocked on Dr. Sarnic's small hut. From inside the home, a man's voice called out, "Who's – who's here? Leave me alone! Just go away!" When they knocked again, he came to the door, pulled it slightly open and peered out at them. "Oh, I'm sorry. Do I know you?"

Dorkla turned to Davia in disgust. "Let's go, Father," she said, "I can see this guy's a nut case, so it can't be him."

"No, it's him," Davia replied insistently to her. Turning to the figure behind the door, he genially stated, "Sorry to bother you, Dr. Sarnic, but could we ask you something?"

"Oh yes, sure, sure," Dr. Sarnic answered absentmindedly. "Please come in," he added as he opened the door and gestured for them to enter. "I just don't get many visitors, you know. I thought maybe you were one of *them*."

"Excuse me," Dorkla interrupted, "Now what do you mean by that?"

Dr. Sarnic sighed. "Long story," as they headed deeper into his hut. Turning to them, he asked, "Now what – what do you want?"

Davia pulled the ring out of his pocket and showed it to Dr. Sarnic. "Well, we were wondering if you could tell us about this ring," as Dorkla took it from her father's and gave it to Dr. Sarnic to examine more closely.

Dr. Sarnic peered closely at the ring, turning it this way and that as Davia had done earlier. "My, my, I see. I haven't seen this for a long time. This is a – a promise ring," he informed them.

"What's a promise ring?" Dorkla asked, puzzled.

Dr. Sarnic replied, "Oh, it's something you give your companion to let them know you'll wait until marriage before you..." Davia quickly covered Dorkla's ears with his hands as Dr. Sarnic continued. "...have sex."

Dorkla pulled away from her father and gave him an angry look. "What did you do that for?" she demanded. "I didn't get to hear what he said!"

"That was the point," Davia answered patiently. "You didn't need to know at your age." Turning to Dr. Sarnic, he asked, "Doctor, is that it? Is it just a promise ring, or is there more?"

Still turning it around, Dr. Sarnic held the ring up to the light. "Yes, yes, of course," he said. "The ring has supernatural abilities and gives special powers if worn for twenty-four hours."

"Right. You must be joking, aren't you?" Davia exclaimed in disbelief.

Dorkla chimed in, "See, Father, I told you he's insane!"

Davia stood up. "Maybe you're right, Dorkla," he answered. "Let's go."

Dr. Sarnic jumped up and blocked their path. "No, wait!" he cried. "Don't go yet!" He handed the ring back to Dorkla. "I'm not joking, because I ended up with powers myself. I can heal people, which is why I'm a doctor. That's why I thought you were going to adultnap me!" He began pacing around.

Dorkla looked puzzled again. "What's adultnap mean?"

"Well, it would make no sense to say kidnap, would it?" answered the doctor. "I'm sure not a kid anymore, not at age fifty-four."

Davia moved towards the hut's door. "Good point," he said. "Thank you for the information, but we really should just get going." They bade the kind but eccentric doctor good-bye to and took their leave.

While they were heading outside, Dr. Sarnic peered out the door and looked left and right down his street before he closed the door behind them.

"Did he say the ring was magical?" Dorkla inquired as they headed back home.

"No," answered Davia. "I mean yes, but he doesn't mean that kind of hocus-pocus nonsense."

They passed by the same pawnshop in Kodaya and contemplated whether they should sell the ring or not. It was really up to Dorkla to decide, since it now belonged to her. "No, I've changed my mind," Dorkla decided. "Let's wait until I at least try testing it before we'll get rid of it."

"What do you mean by getting rid of it?" Davia wanted to know. "We need the money. Dorkla, we're already getting low on food. And what do you mean by testing it?"

"Well, he said it gives you special powers. Don't you want to find out if it's true? I'll wear it for twenty-four hours, and we'll see if anything happens. If nothing happens, we'll sell it, okay?" Dorkla asked in a hopeful voice.

They were halfway between Kodaya and the castle when Davia stopped and said, "Whoa, hold on. Wait a minute before you put that on. Didn't you see how paranoid that guy was? I don't want you acting like him." Davia frowned at the thought.

Dorkla looked at him defiantly. "Well, how do you know if we get the same powers or not? We'll just have to wait and see, right?"

Davia sighed deeply. "If you say so," he replied.

As it was dark by the time they reached the castle, they missed the dinner hour and were so tired they went straight to bed; however, there also wasn't much food left in the castle. Rain fell softly during the night, but Dorkla slept through it. Her dreams were pleasant, too. Before she went to bed, she put the ring on her finger, saying to herself, "Here goes nothing!"

Davia felt from the beginning that she was wasting her time with this foolishness in thinking a ring could possibly possess any sort of power. To him, it was simply that. A ring and nothing more. Apparently, Dorkla had more faith in the unbelievable, but Davia was losing his patience when it came to Dorkla, having not seen her for so long. Putting up with her attitude and ways was something new for someone who had long been nothing more than a slave. But Davia had more respect for his daughter than his owner. He might have never been whipped or beaten, but he sure did miss his freedom, which didn't come easily, wasting away many years of his life, cheapening it away by being just a servant because of Amelia. He didn't hate her for selling him, he was used to being sold since birth. He knew why she did it but didn't appreciate being someone's property, to be bought and sold at someone's whims.

Chapter Seventeen

Reliving the Past

Morning was now approaching. The sun began its upward path in a crystal-clear blue sky. The birds were merrily chirping their morning song and dew made bright drops on the green grass as Dorkla and Davia rose. Dorkla, feeling something different on her hand, looked down, remembering that she still had the promise ring on her middle finger. When she came down the stairs, she was disappointed to only discover milk and a slice of plain bread for breakfast. "That's it? That's all we have to eat?" she complained.

"Well, I told you we were getting low on food," Davia replied. "That, of course, is why I was hoping you were going to sell that ring, but you wanted to keep it, thinking it's going to give you special powers by wearing that silly thing."

Dorkla looked down at the ring, then at her father. "I'm only going to keep it until tonight, then we'll go sell it like I intended," she answered.

"That's all right for now," Davia retorted sarcastically. "We'll just starve to death. Besides, it looks pretty on you. Are you saving yourself for someone?"

Dorkla's face began to darken in anger. "What are you talking about?" she demanded. "It's just a magic ring!" she added, correcting her father.

"Yeah, sure, right, Dorkla," Davia carelessly replied. "Whatever you say. So it is true that we're just going to waste away the day waiting for that ridiculous ring of yours to work?"

Dorkla didn't answer her father. She sat down in a chair and began drinking her milk before giving Davia a reply. She ignored her bread, as it didn't stimulate her appetite at all. "Well, I've been wondering what else my mother wrote in her diary," she finally stated.

At her words, Davia went to Amelia's room and picked up the diary. He returned to the kitchen and dropped it hard on the table. "Sure, here you go," he said, "but don't expect to find out anything important." Davia chuckled.

"We'll see about that," Dorkla replied as she opened the book, flipping through the pages. She flipped to an earlier entry, which revealed some of Amelia's past:

"Dear Diary,

Today was a nice day out in the yard. I cleaned the castle well, so most of my chores are finished. The only thing that could ruin the day was putting up with King Davia's mouth. He always opens it at exactly the wrong time. Lucky I don't plan on whipping him. We might be having a child soon if everything goes to plan due to my sinful thoughts. If it's a boy, I'll name him Xanadu, and if it's a girl, it'll be Dorka. I pity bringing a life into this wretched world of hunger, thirst, pain, sorrow and death. I really didn't want to continue such a cycle of madness. But I should have thought of that before I opened my legs."

"Um, Dorkla?" Davia's voice interrupted her reading that entry. "Maybe you should read a different page." Turning away from her and pacing, he continued, "See? I told you we didn't get along!"

"Sure, Father," Dorkla replied absently, as she turned to another page in the middle of the book:

"Dear Diary,

Where did I go wrong? I had a girl. A miserable, whiny brat. I'm doomed as a parent, I know it. Xanadu seemed like a better name to me. Too bad. I guess I'm stuck with her. Plus she leaks smelly urine. I wish I didn't have her and could give her back."

Dorkla looked down at the book, both thoughtful and hurt at the same time. "I think I'll read another page," she finally said. "Does she always have to complain about me?" She turned a few more pages and began again:

"Dear Diary,

What am I doing here? I can't possibly have a life anymore with a child and a castle in the middle of nowhere. Maybe I should get rid of Davia. He's too much baggage to carry around as of now. We'll see. As for Dorkla, she's getting on my bad side. She keeps falling down when she tries to walk. She still can't seem to feed herself without spilling. Also, I swear she's trying to tell me things, but it sounds like she's speaking a different language of something strange like that. Before, she used to sleep all day, now she keeps me awake. So I guess, Diary, she's the only life I have for now. Not much of one, I admit, but I think I'm starting to adore her nonetheless. Now if there was a way to get baby- vomit stains out of my dress."

Dorkla closed the book, saying, "Well, I guess that's it. There's NOTHING really important in the words said that she left behind. No real point to reading it then if I don't get anything out of it."

"Maybe we should read some passages later," Davia suggested gently. "There might still be some information that's worth looking at. You see, your mother did care about you, somewhat at least."

"Yeah, but it's hard to try and shut her up or to get her to stop complaining about me," Dorkla replied in a disgusted tone.

"But child, shouldn't you give up by now on trying to get back at her? She's dead and gone," Davia responded. "Just don't let anything she says get to you, okay? Yes, she had a big mouth, attitude, and was full of angst, but at least she was good-looking."

"Faa-ther, you're not helping things," Dorkla stated flatly. "If she was hearing the words I'm saying, which I hope she does, I'd tell her she's stuck up and was mean to me with the words she spoke and wrote. Why did she hate me so much, Father? How did I get under her skin so much? I never did anything wrong to her! Amelia should know that a lot of what she said, even unintended, still hurt my feelings very much. I'm not really mad at her, I do love her, actually. I know what she said can't be taken back. I just felt that she took advantage of me. She would always take what I said the wrong way, I swear." Tears stung at her eyes.

Davia gently touched her shoulder. "Well, please know that I'm never leaving you, Dorkla." Standing up, he gave her a loving look. "I'm glad we had this talk and chance to get some things off your chest. Maybe you're right, Dorkla. Maybe your mother is listening to your words. But I'm just not too sure, though."

"I'm glad for the times, though, when she did hear what I told her," Dorkla replied, swiping at her eyes. "I just wish she wouldn't have argued or criticized me so much for no absolute reason."

Both Dorkla and Davia realized that it was time to put Amelia's death behind them by trying to find some new friends. They decided to go and visit a faraway village called Yufala, located behind the castle near Sentimint Forest. After walking along a narrow road for awhile, Dorkla realized she was getting tired. "How much farther, Father, do we have to go?"

Davia reached over and gently rubbed her shoulders. "Don't worry, it's not that much farther." He suddenly stumbled, stepping on a loose rock and almost stubbing his foot on another one. He quickly regained his footing, and they resumed their journey.

The village was now in sight. There were some children next to the village well, so Dorkla and Davia were quiet so that they could overhear their conversation.

"But how do we know they even exist, Caleb?" said one girl. "You've lied so many times in the past!"

"I swear, Mia," insisted the boy she called Caleb, "I'm telling the truth! When I was in Sentimint Forest, I saw a glimpse of what looked like an angel hovering in the air." He spoke with a firm intensity.

The girl called Mia looked at him skeptically. "Are you sure you didn't drink too much of your father's wine? You might just be seeing things. I'll believe it when I see it!"

"Come on, Mia," Caleb said in a pleading tone, "where's your faith at?"

Mia answered doubtfully, "I'm not sure I have that much to believe we'll see an actual angel. Aren't they supposed to be in Heaven? Last time I checked, that Bible stuff was just made to scare kids into being good. That I'm going to burn in Hell and that I have to be good to get into Heaven."

"Who's been telling you that mumbo-jumbo?" Caleb queried.

"Jenny, my big sister," Mia stated stubbornly. "She's older and knows what she's talking about. She says this life is really all there is. That nothing you do or say ultimately matters in the end. I don't know if I believe her, but she must be right. She's older than me."

Caleb looked at her defiantly. "Well, if you tell me, Jenny's dumb as bricks and wouldn't know about smarts even if it bit her in the...."

"He-e-yy!" shouted Dorkla, interrupted their conversation as she approached them. "Are you really going on a quest to find an angel? If so, can I come along with you?"

"Sure, I guess you can tag along," Caleb replied, looking curiously at her. "Who are you? I've never seen you around here before."

"I'm Dorkla," she cheerfully answered. "I live in a castle not too far from here," pointing back toward the direction she and Davia had traveled. Turning to her father, she looked up at him pleadingly. "Can I go with them, Father? Please?"

Davia smiled at her. "Sure, but don't get lost. I don't want to have to get a search party looking for everyone!"

Dorkla looked at him, not sure whether to be amused or embarrassed. "Very funny, Father," she replied, giggling. "I'm sure we won't get lost because Caleb knows the way." Turning to Caleb, she added, "Right, Caleb?"

Caleb stood a little straighter. "Of course!" he stated. "I know the paths of the forest like the back of my foot."

Dorkla laughed at his apparent misstatement. "Don't you mean back of your hand?"

Caleb looked indignantly at her. "What is this? You must met me and now you're trying to tell me what I should say?"

"I was just helping," Dorkla answered apologetically. "I didn't mean anything by it, honest."

As they set off for the forest, Davia called out, "When you get back, come back to the village after you're done playing make-believe!"

Caleb, stung by Davia's comment, stopped and turned around to face him. "What are you talking about, mister? We're looking for an actual, real-life, wings-flapping, halo-wearing angel, sir! I don't know where you've been this whole time, but this is sure not what you call baby playtime."

"Just make sure you came back right here when you're done, okay, Dorkla?" Davia asked, ignoring Caleb's protests.

Once everything was all settled, though, the children set off on pursuit of the angel of Sentimint Forest. They set out on the trail adjacent to the village. This path led to the forest.

"See, Mia," Caleb stated just before they entered the forest, "At least Dorkla here has enough sense to believe in angels, don't you, Dorkla?"

"Of course," Dorkla answered quietly. "The angels took my mother away."

"Well, it should be over here that goes into the forest," Caleb indicated, pointing the way with his hand.

As they entered the forest, the canopy of trees quickly dimmed the sunlight, making it very dark, but they had just enough light to easily discern the walking path.

"I forgot to warn everyone that once you step into Sentimint Forest that it gets dark fast," Caleb announced. "It goes from daylight to like nighttime. So I hope you are not afraid of the dark, you two," he stated to the girls.

"Not at all," stated Mia, "I like the nighttime. It's sooo romantic, I'm not scared," she added, grabbing his arm.

"I thought you weren't a scaredy-cat, Mia," Dorkla said in a snide tone.

"Well, I – I just don't want to get lost, that's all," Mia replied nervously. "Plus I need my knight in shining armor to protect me. Won't you, sweetie?" she added, smiling up at Caleb.

Caleb pulled his arm free of Mia's grasp. "I don't know what you've been thinking, and I'm definitely not wearing any armor, that's for sure," he stated, getting annoyed with Mia's attempts at manipulation.

After this interaction, the trio fell silent as they continued their journey through the forest.

Chapter Eighteen

Quest for the Angel

As they made their way along the forest path, they took their time stepping over branches and fallen trees. When they reached a fallen tree, Caleb would help lift Mia over the downed limbs, as Mia was of a short stature. Dorkla and Mia kept asking Caleb how much farther they had to travel. Over and over he patiently responded, "It shouldn't be too much farther." They both began to really doubt Caleb, but a short while later, they both began to see a light getting brighter ahead of them. This was no ordinary light – it seemed to glow as if from an emanation.

"What is that? It's getting brighter!" shrieked Mia.

"Don't you know anything?" Caleb responded impatiently. "It's obviously the angel, you dummy!" They made their way through the thick underbrush that grew into the path as they pushed forward toward the light. Suddenly they found themselves in a clearing. In the middle of the clearing was a large tree stump. Much to their amazement, hovering above the stump was a being surrounded by a large aura of light. It was so bright that they had to put their hands above their eyes to shield them from the intensity of the glow. Just as quickly as the light intensified, it faded away, and as their eyes adjusted to the gloominess of the forest, they saw that the being was a barely-clad fairy still bathed in a soft glow. Although they were excited by this discovery, Caleb was also a little disappointed.

"See? I told you, Caleb, that it couldn't have been an angel!" Mia cried out, shattering the stillness of the clearing.

"How was I supposed to know?" replied Caleb. "Besides, they look identical!"

"She's beautiful and bright," Dorkla interjected in a mystified tone.

"Quiet!" shouted Caleb. "I think she's going to say something!"

The fairy spoke in a soothing, musical voice. "Yes… who are – are you? Have you come to steal me away?"

In an excited but reassuring voice, Caleb responded, "No, not at all. We came to see you. We thought – I mean, I thought – you were an angel. You see, I saw you somewhat a week ago and ran out of the forest very scared."

"You need not be afraid, children," the fairy replied. "I'm harmless. I'll teach you what is right. I'm a light of this world, as many of you are. I'm no angel by any means. I'm just a meager fairy." Her words had a calming effect on the three children.

"Can I ask you, what are you doing here?" Caleb wanted to know.

The fairy laughed, which sounded like small bells pealing. "I suppose I should ask you the same, shouldn't I? But if you must know, everyone changes, and so does everything over time within the wake of what must be done. You should know that yesterday, the present and even tomorrow are basically the same, only changed by our choices. I might have been created a long time ago, but now I'm not sure. You know what? I might have been born out of your imaginations. You see me because you chose to believe so."

"What do you mean, that we see you because we just made you up?" Caleb demanded. "We didn't create you!"

"Are you sure?" asked the fairy. "Mankind has often tried to justify one's own existence. Just imagine the possibilities if you could get everyone in the whole world to believe in what you believe. If you told everyone I existed, think of the chance at hope that would give them. That's why it's mostly children who see me. Most adults are clouded by doubt. They need proof. It would take everything in the world in order to restore their faith in me. That's why some believe in me at first, then turn away over time. I seem like a very childish thing to them."

"Wait a minute, lady," Caleb stated. "You mean you got everyone to believe it because you said it was true?"

"Well, would you have possibly believed any other way?" the fairy responded. "People need hope, they need something to put their faith in, don't they?"

"Maybe you're right," Caleb answered thoughtfully, "but how do I know if you're even here if I just imagined you?"

"You see me, don't you?" the fairy replied as she lowered her hand towards Caleb. "Feel my hand. It may be great that you see me and still believe, but greater isn't it that there are others who haven't who believe. They are most blessed."

As Caleb gingerly touched her hand, his eyes grew wide. "Your skin is soft like a baby's bottom. But tell me," as he pulled his hand away, "why are you here?"

"You are so full of questions and empty dreams," the fairy answered. "My name is Starlight Starbright."

"Yeah, yeah, Starlight Starbright, first wish I make tonight," Caleb stated in a sarcastic tone. "You didn't answer my question."

Starlight looked at him and replied in an amused voice, "You sure like asking those questions, don't you? It's always good to ask questions. I can grant you one wish, unlike genies who grant three."

"So you only exist because I believe you do," Caleb said. "Then I wish you'd just disappear."

"Granted," Starlight replied, as she suddenly vanished into thin air.

Caleb, realizing his mistake, cried out, "No-o-o-o, don't leave! I have so many more questions to ask you!"

"All in good time," Mia said, lightly patting Caleb's butt with her hand.

Caleb whirled around to face her. "Will you stop that, Mia?" he screamed. "I swear, you're always trying to get into my pants, you little whore!"

Excited at seeing Starlight but dejected at Caleb's wish, they headed back down the path towards Yufala with quite a story to tell. Halfway on the way back, Dorkla giggled, "Well, you did learn something, after all, from Starlight."

"What's that, Dorkla?" Caleb inquired.

"It's you should be careful what you wish for," Dorkla replied, laughing out loud.

"Serves you right, Caleb," Mia added petutantly.

"Shut up and to Hell with you, which is where you'll end up if you die!" Caleb angrily retorted.

"What? Because I don't believe in angels?" Mia responded. "I've been there and done that. Besides, if I go there, I'm taking you with me, you sweet thing. You'll keep me company, won't you?" she added with mock sweetness.

"Don't count on it," Caleb returned. "Angels do too exist. We just didn't see one, that's all. Plus I get enough time spent with you on earth, don't worry me about eternity."

"I don't know about you two, but I'm going to Heaven," Dorkla interrupted. "Because I believe in Jesus Christ."

They fell silent at that point and continued on their way out of Sentimint Forest. Just before they reached the forest edge, however, Mia tripped over a big branch, falling and cutting her leg.

"We got to get her help. We can't just leave her here!" Dorkla cried out. "Plus the cut is kind of deep!"

"Okay, okay, all right, fine," Caleb replied crossly. "If it makes you feel better. I was thinking about just completely leaving her here. At least then she'll have some furry friends like rabbits, bears and ssnakesss." He bent down and picked Mia up.

"Funny!" Mia cried out sarcastically in spite of her pain.

Dorkla looked at the gash on Mia's leg. "She's bleeding pretty badly," she informed Caleb.

Once he had a good hold on Mia, they turned and continued leaving the forest. As they left the forest edge, it became lighter, but as the sun was beginning to set, the light was beginning to fade as they reached the village. Caleb carried Mia to the village healing center, where the doctors there took care of her. Caleb set her down on a bed, and the doctors bandaged up her wound.

"Now she's going to need some rest, you two, so please come back tomorrow," one of the nurses informed Caleb and Dorkla.

"Will she be okay?" asked Caleb anxiously.

Mia gathered up her strength at Caleb's words to respond. "See, my sweetums does care about me, after all!"

"She'll be fine," the nurse told the children. "She just needs some bed rest and soup."

"Nooo, not soup," Mia protested.

Caleb turned to go. "Thank you for your help. We'll be leaving now, so make sure you give Mia plenty of soup," he added sarcastically.

"Bye, Mia, get well soon!" Dorkla called.

"Before we leave, though, how is Mia going to be okay tomorrow?" asked Caleb. "That's not a lot of time."

"Well, that's easy," the nurse answered. "Dr. Sarnic's coming in the morning to help heal her. They say that he even has special powers to do so."

"Those people are probably liars, though," Caleb said to Dorkla. " I know of no such thing. Let's go, Dorkla. Special powers – is she crazy? First I think I'm seeing fairies, now this. Maybe I should go home and lie down."

As they left the healing center, it was getting dark and cold outside. "I have to go after my father," Dorkla stated. "He must be getting worried sick."

"Are you sure?" Caleb asked "I thought you were going to wait and see if Mia will be all right."

"I'm sure," Dorkla responded. "I believe Mia's going to be fine, but I'll pray for her just in case. See you, Caleb!" she called out as she walked away from him. "Maybe we'll meet again someday!"

"Here's hoping so!" called Caleb as Dorkla ran off.

Dorkla had difficulty finding her father. He wasn't where he was when they took off for the forest earlier, so she thought he must be in someone's house. After some searching, Dorkla decided to rest next to the well, hoping her father would return to the place where they'd met Mia and Caleb.

A short while later, Davia made his way back to the well. Bending over Dorkla, he said quietly but urgently, "Get up, Dorkla. We have to go right now."

As she stood up, Dorkla answered, "Yes, Father, I know. But why so soon? We just got here. Can't we at least stay a while longer?"

Pulling on her arm to drag her down the path towards the castle, Davia replied, "No, we can't. We shouldn't have come here at all in the first place. Now let's just leave, okay? I'll fill you in on all the details later." He strode off with a firm grip on Dorkla's arm, with Dorkla straining to keep up with her father's fast pace.

When they were a considerable distance from the village, Dorkla began questioning Davia. "Why did we have to leave so quickly, Father? What was it you wanted to tell me? I hope it's important. So please tell me already!"

Davia suddenly stopped and released his grip on Dorkla's arm and turned to face his daughter. "Well, if you so have to know, Little Smarty Pants, since you have to know everything, it just so happens that somebody has possibly caught on to us.

Dorkla looked up at her father, a puzzled look on her face. "What? What are you referring to?"

"Do I have to explain what you should have already realized? We might be in big trouble because of what you did." Davia paused, then continued, "So we need to leave this minute before someone catches us."

Dorkla was more confused then before. "What did I do wrong?" she asked.

Davia's patience was at an end. "We'll talk about it once we get far enough away from this place. We can't be speaking or even be seen here anymore, you hear me?" he demanded.

"Yes, Father," Dorkla replied obediently, "but what about Mia and Caleb?" Davia didn't answer, as the path got rather rough at this point and they found themselves stumbling over rocks.

They could make out the silhouette of the castle in the distance through the moonlight, although finding their way was difficult in the darkness. At that point, Dorkla erupted in anger. "Okay, fine! We've made it this far and we've gone far enough. Now speak up and tell me why I'm part of the Blame Game!"

Rolling his eyes in frustration and sighing, Davia said, "All right! Just calm down." He paused for several minutes, gathering his thoughts, before continuing. "It's about Amelia. Some people I overheard said that they were wondering where she was. Some said she was on vacation. Others thought she was what she really is, dead. You know what that means, right? It means she's never coming back. They're going to become curious as to where she's at, you know. I never told them anything. They said some people went to the castle while we were gone and couldn't find her."

Dorkla looked fearful. "Are they still there?" she asked anxiously. "I didn't tell Mia or Caleb anything about Mother."

Davia looked down gently at Dorkla. "I believe you, I really do, even though sometimes you can be a loudmouth. That's why we need to get back to the castle, to find out," he said, although he sounded more confident than he felt.

Chapter Nineteen

Meanwhile, Back at the Castle

They continued on their journey home, being careful to avoid the pointed rocks as they made their way through the darkness towards the castle, hoping that no one was rummaging through their happy home, or what's left of it. Dorkla wondered if they might have been the ones who entered the castle when Amelia and she had gone to Kodaya City the last time she had been out of the castle. As she walked, she fantasized that if she were to encounter an unwanted visitor, she would bash any intruder's head in.

The main door was ajar when they got there, but to their great relief, no one was in the castle. "I'm getting hungry," Dorkla stated with a yawn.

"Tough," Davia flatly replied. "There's nothing left to eat or drink. We're starving because of that morbid ring you love so much."

"Couldn't we just tax the rich and get some money?" Dorkla whined.

"No!" Davia firmly replied. "We're not going to resort to your mother's old lifestyle. Makes me wonder, though, if maybe people are so used to getting taxes collected that now that she isn't, that could be why they're getting suspicious."

"Just let me wear the ring until morning to make sure I've worn it for a full day," Dorkla pleaded. "Then we'll sell it. Because of right now, I feel nothing, so it must not be working yet." Davia sighed, then turned and headed for his room for some long-needed rest and relaxation. Not getting any reply, Dorkla went up to her own room, realizing how spent she was.

After changing into her nightclothes, she climbed into her bed and looked up and out of her bedroom window as she did so. She could see that the night sky was clear, showing a bright full moon and a myriad of stars. Dorkla thought she could see a smiling female face in the moon's soft glow. She always thought of the moon's face as female, as it gave off a much gentler light than the bright sun. Gazing dreamily at the moon and stars, she fell asleep. Her dreams were vivid and involved unicorns, rainbows and fairies.

The morning sun's bright rays helped awaken both Dorkla and Davia. However, the lack of food in the castle didn't help either their stomachs or their dispositions. "Father, my stomach's grumbling," Dorkla whined.

"Well, are you ready to sell that ring of yours?" asked Davia. "You don't happen to have any special powers by now, do you?"

Dorkla looked crestfallen. "No, I don't think so," she admitted. "I guess not. I suppose we can sell it, then." She pulled the ring off her finger and added, "I really got tricked, didn't I? It's phony and false. Promised me nothing, I say."

She handed the ring to Davia, who placed it in one of his pockets. He stood up and said, "Okay, then, let's go."

Dorkla looked down at her attire. "Not yet – I'm still in my nightclothes! I'll just go get changed first." She turned and ran up the stairs to her room to get dressed. Davia sat down as she dashed out of the room, hoping that she wouldn't take too much time doing so. After waiting for awhile, he began pacing the room. It seemed like an eternity, but at last Dorkla re-entered the room, by now fully dressed.

She looked up at her father and brightly asked, "When are we going to church? You'll take me there, right, Father?"

Davia sighed and sat down before replying, "Dorkla, are you serious? You know, there isn't a single church within a thousand miles of here. Do you want a Crusade? You shouldn't be forcing your religion on others by dying by the sword. Keep quiet about that kind of thinking. Did your mother fill your head with those stories and ideas? I've never seen a Bible before, so I don't know how you could have found out about all of that. It doesn't even say anything about God on money, books or anywhere else yet."

Dorkla stubbornly replied, "Well, I felt God pulling at my heart and tugging inside at my feelings since I was a youngster. Maybe just by wondering how we got here. How we were made. I don't need to know about religion to wonder or ask questions, do I?"

Davia thought a minute before answering. "I guess not. That's a lot of thinking for one little girl. But how could you find out about something you know nothing about? If you weren't told, you'd never know at all."

Dorkla chuckled, then replied, "Well, no one told me how or that I need to eat or go potty. I figured that out for myself. Even if somebody had to show me, I would have found out eventually what I needed to do. Same with God. I know I can't see Her, but that doesn't mean I wouldn't have figured out She exists. Even if nobody told me about Her, I would have put two and two together."

Davia laughingly returned, "By the way, God's a He, not a She, you girl." Standing up, he added, "Now let's get going and sell that ring. I'm getting hungrier by the second."

Dorkla sought to correct him by saying, "Don't you mean by the minute, Father? Besides, I'm still learning. I'm not even sure yet if the Earth's flat or round." Davia didn't answer her as they set off for Kodaya.

When they arrived in Kodaya, it was very quiet, as it was still early in the morning and most people were still asleep. They made their way to the little shop and its owner to pawn off the ring. As there were no crowds, they were first in line to do business with the shopkeeper.

Recognizing them, the little shopkeeper cheerfully called out, "So, I see you're back. Planning on giving up the goods?"

Stepping up to the counter, Davia replied, "Yes, we'll sell the ring after all, after much thinking and debating."

The shopkeeper reached under the counter to a coin box and pulled out a handful. Counting them out, he handed them to Davia, stating, "Here you go – 95 coins."

Dorkla's face grew dark with anger. "What? I thought it was a hundred coins!" she shouted.

"You don't expect me to keep the same price forever, do you?" the shopkeeper coolly replied. "I'm running a business here, missy. You keep me waiting, then the price drops." Turning to Davia, he added, "Now, you selling, or no?"

Sighing, Davia handed over the ring. "Okay, fine. You win. We need the money anyway. I've got to sell it before we starve to death," he said dejectedly. The shopkeeper didn't offer his hand for a handshake, not that Davia would have shaken it if offered. He would have more liked to break his hand, not shake it. He snatched the money bag and hurried Dorkla out of the shop, then went to the food shop to get milk and other essentials.

However, the door was locked. Davia knocked, and a burly shopkeeper came and opened it a small distance. "Sorry, we're closed, sir" he said crisply. "Take your business elsewhere, sir."

Davia looked at him in frustration. "What? We just got some money and you're open any minute from now, according to your sign!" he shouted angrily.

The shopkeeper glanced back into the store, then at Davia. "Yes, you're right," he stated. "Now we're open. Thank you for being patient, sir."

"Please quit calling me sir, okay?" Davia retorted. He pushed past the shopkeeper and looked around. Pointing at a few products, he added, "I'll take some of this and some of that." As the shopkeeper bundled and handed the items over to them, Davia handed them over to Dorkla for her to carry. Once the items were paid for, they bade the shopkeeper good-day and headed back home to the castle.

On the way back, Davia had to listen to Dorkla grumbling and complaining about how much she missed the ring and was sad to see it go because she was so used to wearing it and thought it looked rather pretty and cute on her.

Arriving back at the castle, Dorkla carelessly set the food bundles on the table, not caring if they were put away or not. She didn't care anymore now that her ring was gone. She just plopped herself down on a kitchen chair, pouting.

Davia looked at her and smiled, saying in a happy tone, "Cheer up. We have food now!"

"Yes, but no ring," Dorkla replied gloomily. Standing up and turning towards the door, she added, "I'm not hungry anymore, so I think I'll just go lie down for awhile."

"Suit yourself," Davia answered, "but I'm hungry. Besides, that crummy ring was worthless anyway. It was idiotic to become attached to it."

Dorkla didn't reply; she headed up to her room. But sleep eluded her. She found herself becoming uncomfortable, restlessly tossing and turning, feeling rather warm. Maybe I'm sick, she thought. But that can't possibly be it. She felt no other symptoms, no coughing or vomiting. Not being sure, she got out of bed to ask Davia, finding him still in the kitchen.

"Father, I think there's something wrong with me. Maybe I'm getting sick or dying because I'm very hot." She grabbed Davia's hand and pressed it to her forehead. He gently touched her forehead and the sides of her neck, looking thoughtful.

"I guess all we can do is go visit the doctor," Davia suggested.

"No, don't tell me. Not that lunatic guy, Dr. Sarnic. Why him?" Dorkla inquired.

"Well, if something's wrong with you, maybe he can heal you. He has powers, remember?" Davia prodded.

Dorkla looked at him doubtfully. "How can you be sure? When the ring didn't give me any powers? He must be lying to us then."

"Well, whether he has special powers or not, we're going to see him because you need a doctor and maybe he has medicine to treat you," Davia stated firmly.

Since Kodaya was on the way to Cilowick, Davia decided to buy some ice for cooling down Dorkla's warm skin, so he bought a bucket of ice and put some of it in a cloth bag. "This should do the trick," Davia said as he gently pressed the ice bag to Dorkla's forehead. Dorkla held the ice to her head as they traveled out of Kodaya and into Cilowick, feeling a small amount of water trickle down her face as the ice began to melt. Having spent the last of the money, it was sure they would go hungry once the food was entirely consumed.

Arriving at Dr. Sarnic's house, they knocked on his door, but no one answered. "That's odd," Davia pondered out loud. "He never leaves the house. Beats me why he would be gone." Dorkla pushed the door open, and they both went inside.

They both nearly jumped from fright seeing the doctor hiding behind the door. "What are you doing?" Dorkla demanded. "I nearly had a heart attack being scared like that!"

"Please – take anything you want," Dr. Sarnic whispered in a quivering voice. Recognizing them, he said in a relieved tone, "Oh, it's you. What are you doing here? You're not going to adult-nap me, are you?"

Davia sighed. "Of course not," he replied soothingly. "I sure hope you don't treat all your guests like this. Now, the reason we're here is because Dorkla's sick. Something's wrong with her after she wore that ring of yours. So can you tell me what's wrong with her?" he added anxiously.

Dr. Sarnic turned his attention to Dorkla and answered, "Yes, sure – and it's not my ring. Let's just get that out of the way. It's certainly not a fever, that's for sure." While he was talking, he placed his hands on her forehead, cheeks and both sides of her neck.

"Then what is it?" Davia asked in a worried tone. "We didn't come all this way for no reason."

Dr. Sarnic turned to face Davia. "It's winter fever," he stated, "must be the power the ring gave her."

Davia's face grew dark with anger. "What kind of power?" he demanded. "She's burning up here! We almost used up a bucket of ice."

Dr. Sarnic stood up, took the bucket and filled it with water. He then placed the bucket in front of Dorkla. Taking her hand, he placed it on the water. Suddenly, the water turned into a bucket of solid ice.

"Remarkable!" Dr. Sarnic exclaimed. "Why didn't I see it before?"

"So what?" Davia replied carelessly. "All she did was turn water into ice. I mean, oh my goodness, how did you do that, Dorkla?"

Dr. Sarnic looked patiently at Davia. "You see, that's her power, but all power has a bad side effect. In your daughter's case, she generates too much body heat and will have to live in cold temperatures."

"Like where?" Davia demanded. "She's just a little girl! She can't live alone!"

"She must," Dr. Sarnic calmly replied," because what if her powers possibly end up in the wrong hands? There's an ice cave east of here, an igloo of sorts. She can live there. There's a lot of food stored there."

"No way!" Davia shouted. Turning towards the door, he added, "We're leaving!" Seizing Dorkla's arm, he strode angrily out the door of the doctor's home, with Dorkla almost tripping in her efforts to keep up.

On the way home, they ran out of ice, as trying to keep Dorkla cool melted it all. At one point, Dorkla collapsed from heat exhaustion, even though the outside temperatures were not very warm. Davia gently picked her up and carried her home. When they reached the castle's moat, Dorkla reached out her hand and touched the water, freezing the entire moat instantly. She then wriggled free of her father's arms and laid down on top of the ice, cooling herself down.

Watching Dorkla's actions and how it relieved her heat exhaustion, Davia sighed and stated, "This is worse than I thought. We can't stay here. We're going to where that crazy kook told us." Leaving Dorkla on the icy moat for her own comfort, Davia ran into the castle and gathered all of Dorkla's meager clothes and belongings in a basket along with the few possessions he had.

Scooping Dorkla back into his arms and balancing the basket, they returned to Dr. Sarnic's house, and Davia wearily told the doctor, "Okay, you win. Now where is that cave at?" By this time, Davia's arms were aching from carrying Dorkla for such a long distance.

Chapter Twenty

Ice Cavern

Dr. Sarnic smiled. "I'm glad you came back in time. There's something I forgot to tell you before you left."

"What is it?" Davia asked, very puzzled. "We don't have all day. Tell me, if it's important!"

"Yes, yes. I forgot to inform you that unless your daughter lives in a cold climate, living in warm or hot temperatures might kill her eventually." Dr. Sarnic looked grim.

"Now you tell me that now my girl is cursed with an incurable disease just because she wore that miserable godforsaken ring you gave her? Why did you give it to her in the first place if you knew it would have that effect?" Davia's voice grew louder as he spoke.

"It's called winter fever, and I'm sure every fever might possibly have a cure," the doctor patiently replied. "If it does, I don't know what it is. Maybe somebody knows. For now, we have to get going before she gets more ill."

"Fine then," Davia stated impatiently. "Let's go. But after we bring her there, I'm going to search for a cure. I'll ask somebody, like you said. I'll do whatever it takes to make her better."

Davia picked Dorkla up once again, and the three travelers headed out of Dr. Sarnic's house towards the path leading eastward to the ice cave. Dr. Sarnic then pulled a map out of his travel bag to aid in their journey, saying cheerfully, "It's been awhile since I've been out of Cilowick, so I'm not exactly sure where we're at or going."

Davia sighed heavily and coughed from the cold air. "We're getting closer, I can tell. It's east, right? If you can heal people, why can't you cure her?"

Rolling up the map and putting it back into his bag, Dr. Sarnic answered, "I can heal sick people of regular illnesses, not something caused by a ring." Davia didn't reply to this, and they traveled for quite a distance with not a word spoken between them.

After a considerable amount of time, they reached their destination, the ice cave. Carefully stepping inside, they discovered a chair made completely of ice, upon which Davia gently set Dorkla to rest. "I shall now call thee Snow Princess Dorkla," Dr. Sarnic stated.

Davia grinned. "What is this?" he playfully demanded. "You meet my daughter for a few minutes and now you're renaming her?"

Dorkla looked anxiously up at Davia. "You're not leaving, Father, are you? I'm feeling better, honest."

Davia knelt beside her and gently stroked her hair. "That's good, honey, but we need to go. We're going to look for a cure to make you not sick anymore. Okay? Then I'll be back to get you." He stood up as if to leave.

Dr. Sarnic gently patted her arm and added, "Now don't leave this cave until it's winter, or you're surely die. And remember to return by winter's end."

Davia bent down and kissed Dorkla's cheek good-bye, and Dr. Sarnic and he left the cave to head back to Cilowick. "I hope I can remember the way back to my house," Dr. Sarnic confided to Davia.

"That makes two of us," Davia replied, not feeling very good for having to leave his daughter behind. "I need to get home myself. So Doctor, where can I find someone who may know about a cure for Dorkla's ailment?"

Dr. Sarnic looked thoughtful. "I don't know," he finally said, "someone in Kodaya could know something. I heard once that someone there had a similar brief connection to the ring, getting super powers."

"Good," Davia answered, feeling a bit relieved, "that's on the way. I'll stop by after I leave you. Really then," he added, "what's his power?"

"Funny you should ask, Davey," Dr. Sarnic said. "Is that your name? Did I get that right? I'm no good with people's names. Anyway, you see, he can't really hear or talk."

"What?" Davia exclaimed in amazement. "What kind of a power is that supposed to be? That's not really a helpful thing. So how am I supposed to even communicate with him?"

"I didn't say it was a good thing," Dr. Sarnic replied evenly. "That's the bad side effect. I'm not sure what the good power was that he inherited though, because he didn't tell me. I could only figure out what his side effect was, as I'm a doctor and only I could figure out that kind of diagnosis. The only way to talk to him is using sign language or writing things down on paper for him to read."

At that point, they arrived at Dr. Sarnic's house. Davia thanked him for his assistance and bade him good-bye as he continued on to Kodaya City, where there were many people and knowing it was going to be difficult to find the person for whom he was searching.

As he entered Kodaya City, a memory came back to Davia. "I remember being taught some signing language when I was young," he mused out loud, "but I can only make alphabet letters. Maybe I could get his attention by doing a few hand signs." He stretched his hands high in the air above his head, and as he did so, he looked around and noticed a few eyes were drawn to this odd spectacle. Using both hands to form block letters as best as he could, he spelled out, "H-E-L-P."

Strangely enough, this rudimentary effort worked. Out of the small crowd strode a dark-haired man directly toward Davia, who nodded in understanding as he neared him. The stranger tried to use his own hands to "talk" to Davia, but he was spelling so quickly that Davia couldn't keep up. Davia held up his hand to stop the man from continuing, then reached into his bag, drawing out a piece of parchment and a small box containing a quill pen and a stoppered bottle of ink. Stepping over to a table and motioning the stranger to follow, Davia set the parchment and box down on the table. He opened the box and removed the quill pen and ink bottle, then unstoppered the ink. Dipping the quill into the ink, Davia bent over the parchment, then wrote:

"Sorry – I don't know enough about making hand signs to communicate well with you."

Davia looked at the man, and the stranger again nodded his head in understanding. Davia bent back over the parchment and continued:

"Can you help me? I need to find a cure for my daughter. She's cursed from a Promise Ring she wore. Do you know what the cure is?"

As Davia straightened and looked at him pleadingly, the stranger nodded his head, took the quill pen from Davia, and bent over the parchment to write:

"Come back tomorrow and I'll tell you."

Davia nodded his head. He restoppered the ink bottle and carefully put the bottle and the quill pen back inside their storage box. He then rolled the parchment back up and placed both back inside his travel bag. Turning away from the stranger, he headed back home to the castle.

Once he entered the castle, he prepared and ate some of the food Dorkla and he had purchased earlier in the day – it had seemed like an eternity ago. Feeling exhausted, he went to his room to get some sleep; however, sleep eluded him. He couldn't help but worry about Dorkla's well-being. He wondered how he ever lived without her when he was a slave. His years of slavery were a time he wished he could forget, but it was still a dark, painful memory. Even not spending time with someone doesn't make it any easier. After what seemed like hours, Davia finally drifted off to sleep.

Davia awakened to bright sunlight warming his face. As he became more aware of where he was, he realized that he'd slept in because Dorkla wasn't there to wake him up. As comfortable as the bed felt, he knew he had to get up to find the stranger and discover what he had to tell him about helping Dorkla.

Davia quickly finished off a breakfast of eggs and bread. He worried about whether he'd run out of food soon. Maybe Amelia had some money lying around somewhere, he thought to himself. He went into her room to check it out, but all he could find was that demented diary of hers. Even though he needed to go see the stranger, he decided to read some of it. Most of the pages complained about Dorkla, but one page caught his eye, as it had the word "money" on it. He read:

"Dear Diary,

I hate to keep secrets, but I must confess my sins of greed. I've been hiding and hoarding my money. I don't want Dorkla to get it; if she found it, she might waste it on sweets and God only knows what. So I'm hiding the money in the secret room that's locked, and only I have the key. I'm not telling anyone where the key is except for you, Diary. You can keep a secret, right? It's under the bottom leg of my bed."

Davia was scarcely able to breathe, he was so excited at this revelation. He closed the diary and went over to the bed. Lifting up the leg of the bed, he discovered, sure enough, that the key was there. He quickly picked it up, then let the leg drop to the floor with a loud "clunk." Now where was this "secret room?" he wondered.

He crossed Amelia's room and opened one door, but it was only a closet. Then he remembered that there was a door in Dorkla's room that had never seemed to be open when he was in there. Bounding up the stairs two at a time, he reached Dorkla's room very quickly. Is this it? he thought to himself. The key fit easily into the slot, but rust inside the lock made turning it very difficult. Davia strained to turn the key, and before long it snapped in two inside the lock. However, it was enough to unlock the door, and it slowly swung open with a screeching sound.

To Davia's awe and amazement, the room was filled with money.

Chapter Twenty-One

Davia's Trial

Lots of it, actually. There were gold, silver and bronze coins that glittered and sparkled. Davia's eyes grew wide as he realized he'd struck it rich. There was more than enough for food and to live on.

****

Back at the ice cave, Dorkla awakened even later in the morning than her father had. Had she been hibernating? she thought to herself. She realized she had been sleeping on a bed of ice, but she didn't feel cold at all for some reason. Normally in this climate, she would have frozen to death.

****

Davia's admiration for all his sudden wealth was interrupted by a loud rapping resonating from the castle's heavy iron door knockers. Now who could that be? he wondered to himself. I'm not expecting any visitors. Maybe it's the stranger who can't talk, he thought hopefully. But how could he find where I live? Humph – maybe he followed me home. That could be it.

However, once he opened the door, his heart sank. There stood the local sheriff and some of his men. What could they possibly want? he asked himself.

The sheriff loudly proclaimed, "Sir, you are under arrest for the murder of Queen Amelia!"

"What are you talking about?" Davia asked the men. "I didn't kill her. I'm innocent, I tell you!"

"Tell it to the judge," the sheriff replied flatly. "We were looking around outside when we found a grave. We dug it up and found her body, which we will give a proper royal burial at a later time. So if you didn't kill her, who did?"

Davia gulped, realizing to admit the truth would get Dorkla into trouble. Not wanting to do that, he decided to take the blame for it. He stood there silently until the sheriff impatiently shouted, "All right, away with him!" The men seized Davia, put him in irons and carried him off to prison, awaiting his trial in front of the judge. After languishing in a dark, damp prison cell for a few days, he was brought before the Court.

Judge Connoly pounded his gavel as the bailiff loudly announced, "Hear ye, hear ye! Court is now in session."

The judge looked down his bench at Davia. "How do you plead?" he asked in a weary voice.

Before he could answer, the prosecutor interrupted, "Your Honor, can I have permission to question the defendant?"

"Yes, you may," the judge replied, "I don't see why not."

The prosecutor puffed himself up and strutted between Davia and the judge's bench. Whirling to face Davia, he pointed his long, bony finger at him and asked, "Mr. Davia, did you or did you not murder Queen Amelia?"

Davia looked straight ahead as he spoke in a firm, clear tone. "I can neither confirm nor deny the allegations, but I take all the blame."

The prosecutor turned away from Davia with a smug look on his face. "No further questions, Your Honor," he stated.

The lawyer appointed to represent Davia stood up and stated, "I'd like to call Davia's first witness." Turning to the gallery, he said, "Dr. Sarnic, please come forward to the stand."

Dr. Sarnic timidly stood up and slowly made his way to the front of the Courtroom. After being seated, Davia's lawyer continued in a pleasant tone, "Dr. Sarnic, do you know why we are here today?"

Dr. Sarnic yawned and replied, "Actually, I really don't. Do you mind telling me so I can go home and get back to sleep?"

Davia's attorney leaned towards him and asked, "Did you know, Doctor, that your friend Davia is on trial for manslaughter?"

Dr. Sarnic looked shocked. "Oh, my no, I didn't! I guess now I know I might have been next!" Chaos erupted in the Courtroom at his exclamation.

"Order in the Court! Order in the Court!" shouted Judge Connoly, pounding his gavel several times. Once order was restored, he continued, "We'll have a brief recess so that the jury can deliberate and make their decision."

Back in his cell, Davia paced nervously, wondering what the outcome would be. He kept thinking of Dorkla and that there would be no one to take care of her. He also wondered about the mute man and that he hadn't been able to get an answer to what could cure Dorkla. He would never be given the chance if he ended up in prison for a long time, possibly for life, or even if he had to forfeit his.

It seemed like forever before the guards returned to take him back to the Courtroom. Once inside, the judge returned and pounded his gavel as the bailiff announced, "Hear ye, hear ye! Court is back in session."

Davia was nervous and sweating as he awaited the Court's decision, wondering what the verdict would be. He was fearful of the outcome. What was he thinking about, he wondered, taking the blame for Dorkla's misdeed. The only reason he even did it was because of how much he loved his daughter. He couldn't bear to see Dorkla rotting her life away in prison. It was better that it be him so that Dorkla could live her life the rest of her days. Besides, she would probably die due to the condition she currently has. He couldn't possibly let that happen.

After a whispered conversation between the foreman and Judge Connoly, the judge cleared his throat and bade Davia to stand. Looking steadily at Davia, he announced, "The jury has found Davia to be guilty of the charges of murdering Queen Amelia. Unless he pays the amount of one thousand gold coins, he will be serving a sentence of twenty-five years in the Kodaya Prison."

Davia was shocked and surprised by the verdict and by finding out that Kodaya even had a prison, as he had never seen it before. It must have been located behind the shops or even hidden, he thought to himself. Leaning over towards Dr. Sarnic, Davia pleaded, "Dr. Sarnic, please tell Dorkla where I am, that I miss and love her, and please take care of her for me."

Dr. Sarnic gave Davia a reassuring smile as he was hauled back to prison, knowing what he had to do to honor Davia's requests.

Back in his dank, dark cell, Davia had little to do but think. From time to time he was brought some food, mostly thin soup or gruel in a wooden bowl, and if he was lucky he got a piece of dark bread to go with it, but seldom any fruit or cheese. He tried to keep his mind active, as he knew that he would sink into despair if he didn't.

****

Back in her ice cave, Dorkla had little to do as the days slowly went by. She would pretend that icicles were dolls and she would play house with them, but like her father in his prison cell, she fought off boredom every day.

Upon leaving the Courthouse, Dr. Sarnic went home to Cilowick to get some sleep, and for a few days forgot about Davia's requests. On the third day, however, he remembered his promise and set out to visit Dorkla, who was getting sick of being shut away in her cave.

As he approached the cave, Dr. Sarnic saw her sitting on her ice chair wearing a white fur coat. He had given her that coat a while back in case she got cold, a silly thing to think, considering she is living in a cave made of ice. As he got closer, he could see the look on her face indicated she was bored and depressed.

Dr. Sarnic put a smile on his face as he said, "Cheer up, Princess Dorkla, because I've brought you some good news!"

"What, is a savior born today in a manger? Possibly named Jesus?" Dorkla asked sarcastically.

"No, not really," Dr. Sarnic replied. "I have some news about your father, Davia."

Dorkla's face brightened. "Oh, goody, goody!" she exclaimed. "So he's gotten the cure and he's coming to visit me?"

"Sorry, no," Dr. Sarnic gently answered. "Maybe I should have started with the bad news,"

Dorkla's face fell. "What? You never mentioned that!" she shouted angrily. "Is he all right? He's not hurt, is he?" A frightened expression crept across her face.

"No, not at all, thank goodness," Dr. Sarnic reassured her. "Where did you get that kind of an idea? He's fine, but sadly, he's in prison. They think he killed..."

"It's Amelia, isn't it?" Dorkla interrupted. "I had a feeling. He didn't kill her. Someone else did."

Dr. Sarnic let out a sigh of relief. "Oh, my, you mean that?" he asked. "Davia's innocent of the charges against him. But that's sure a dilemma if I ever did see one."

Dorkla stood up and said, "It is, isn't it? If only I could speak to my father. Maybe I could find out a way to get him out. Maybe you could talk to him!" Her face brightened at the thought.

"I guess I could give it a try," Dr. Sarnic replied. "Just make sure you stay here and be a good girl." Turning toward the cave entrance, he added, "I hope you're right. Maybe there is a way."

"I will, but please don't be gone for very long. I need someone to talk to so that I don't go insane. All right?" Dorkla added anxiously.

Dr. Sarnic gave her a quick hug and bade her good-bye. After leaving the cave, he headed home to prepare himself for the visit to the prison, then made his way there to talk to Davia about finding a way to get him out of prison that didn't involve a prison break. Once he reached the prison, Dr. Sarnic found that visits aren't normally allowed, but he was able to talk his way in to speak to Davia.

Upon seeing him, Davia's face was wreathed in smiles, and his great relief was evident as well. "I'm so glad you're here!" he exclaimed to the doctor. "You don't know what this means to me. Did you do what I asked you to do? Did you speak to Dorkla?"

Dr. Sarnic smiled and patted his arm. "Yes I did, and she told me something. She said that you're innocent, which I hoped was true because you don't look like the violent type to me." Leaning towards Davia and looking straight into his eyes, he added, "Is it true? Because I'd have to hear you say it to make sure."

Davia returned the doctor's steely gaze. "Of course, I didn't do it," he answered in a firm voice. "So is Dorkla all right?" he added anxiously.

"She's fine. A little cold and sad," Dr. Sarnic replied. "And she asked me to ask you if there might be a way to get you out."

Davia paused. "Hmm – let me think a moment." Brightening, he added, "There might be one way. If they're paid the amount needed, I can get out. That's it!" he shouted. "Can you go to my castle? In a room there's a lot of money. If you go to this room and bring one thousand gold coins, the amount they are charging me, I can be set free." Pointing in the castle's direction, he added in a pleading tone, "The castle's just up the road from here. Hurry!"

Before Dr. Sarnic could give an answer, the guards dragged Davia back to his cell, leaving it in faith for him to do the right thing. One of the guards told Dr. Sarnic, "Sorry. Visiting hours are over, and you have to leave."

Hurrying out of the prison, Dr. Sarnic turned and headed up the road from Kodaya City to the castle. Once he reached it, he timidly knocked on one of the heavy wooden doors, then realized that no one was there to answer. Cautiously, he pushed the door open. Peering into the large entry room, he saw that the room was completely empty. Wandering through the cavernous rooms of the castle, Dr. Sarnic was beginning to wonder if he was ever going to find this "money room" Davia had described, as he had never been inside the castle before.

After much searching, Dr. Sarnic finally found the hidden money room. He almost fainted from the sight of so much money. He took a few deep breaths, then began scooping and counting the gold coins. Once he had enough, he placed them in cloth bags and with great effort, carried them back to the prison. Knowing how much money he had as well as how much was in the room, he was initially reluctant to hand over the bags to bail Davia out, but remembering Dorkla and her sad face, he got up the courage to do so. When the prison officials saw the money, they sent guards to release Davia, who by now was looking sickly pale from a lack of sunlight and proper nutrition.

Blinking in the brightness of daylight after having been in the gloom of the prison, Davia patted Dr. Sarnic's shoulder and said, "You did the right thing. I'm proud of you."

"I almost didn't do the so-called 'right thing,'" Dr. Sarnic admitted rather sheepishly. Being greedy, I wanted to keep the money."

"I understand," Davia replied. "When we get back, I'll give you your fair share for your help."

"Good. I need enough to get paid back for the coat I gave Dorkla," Dr. Sarnic stated in a hopeful voice.

As they returned to the castle, Davia took many deep breaths, grateful to be a free man and savoring the sweet smell of fresh air and the sight of clear blue sky.

Davia stepped onto the familiar stone floors of the castle and announced, "It's good to be home again!" Both men went up to the treasure room in Dorkla's bedroom. Davia grabbed a small cloth pouch and filled it with more than enough coins for Dr. Sarnic, who was rubbing his hands and whose eyes danced with glee at the sight of it all.

After giving many thanks to Davia, Dr. Sarnic took his leave of him and headed back to Kodaya City and Cilowick. Davia was exhausted, as he was unable to get a good night's sleep in prison. He went to lie down in his bed and fell sound asleep.

He awakened much later with a sense that something terrible had happened. Racing up to the treasure room, he stopped dead in his tracks in horror, as it was empty. All of the rest of the money was gone – stolen and vanished. The only person Davia could think of who might have taken it while he was sleeping was Dr. Sarnic. That old, good-for-nothing fat lying thief, he thought to himself. That pig thinks he can steal all my money? Well, I'll show him, Davia kept thinking. All thoughts of trying to find the mute stranger and help Dorkla fled due to his anger at Dr. Sarnic. His only thought was to go to Dr. Sarnic's house and go get his money back.

As he went through Kodaya, the thought occurred to him that he should talk to the mute man, but there was not enough time at that point. Approaching Dr. Sarnic's door, Davia knocked furiously, so much so that the doctor was afraid that someone was there to adult-nap him, as if anyone would want to.

Dr. Sarnic slowly and fearfully opened the door. In a quavering voice, he asked, "Hello? Who's there?" Seeing Davia, he breathed a sigh of relief and added, "Davia, what's wrong? You look stressed."

In reply, Davia grabbed him by the top of his tunic, saying, "You know very well. Where's my money you stole from me?"

Dr. Sarnic tried to push Davia away from him, and in a huffy voice, answered, "I beg your pardon. All I have is the money you gave me. I would never steal from you; you're my friend."

Davia released his grip on the doctor's tunic and said, "Really, you think I'm your friend?"

Dr. Sarnic smiled at Davia as he answered, "Yes, Davia. You're the only real person I know. You're the only actual friend I have."

Davia was speechless for a minute. Then he said, "I never knew you felt like that about me. Here I thought you were just some creepy old guy I was visiting all along. So you really didn't take the money? I guess I believe you after all."

"What are friends for?" Dr. Sarnic asked. "Oh, you want to see the shoes I just bought for Dorkla?" He held up a pair of white doeskin slippers.

"That's okay," Davia replied, "I've got to go." He turned as if to leave, then turned back toward the doctor. "That reminds me that I need to visit Dorkla and ask that man about a cure, so I'd better get going."

"Are you sure?" Dr. Sarnic asked in a pleading tone. "Please stay awhile. I've got tea, cookies and some fresh milk. We could have whatever you want, maybe some meat, cheese and bread."

Davia wasn't listening, as he was already heading out the door. He was mulling over what Dr. Sarnic had said and knew he'd been telling the truth. It would be foolish for someone to steal all that money, then buy his daughter a gift. Oh well, he thought to himself. It's out of my hands, but it was never his anyway. It had belonged to Amelia in the first place, but it never should have been hers either, as all of it was taken from taxing her subjects over time.

"Wait, wait!" Dr. Sarnic shouted, panting to catch up to Davia. "I forgot to give you Dorkla's slippers!"

Taking them from Dr. Sarnic's outstretched hand, Davia smiled and said, "Thank you. I'll make sure she gets them. Now could you please leave me alone?" Turning away from Dr. Sarnic and continuing on towards the ice cave, he thought to himself, I've been spending more time knowing Dr. Sarnic than I was ever planning on.

As he neared the ice cave, Davia's pace quickened, knowing that he was going to see his little daughter whom he hadn't seen a long time. Dorkla could see her father approaching from a distance, getting more and more excited as he neared her. She hadn't seen him a such a long time and she missed him so much.

Once he entered the cave, she threw herself into his arms for a big hug. She wasn't angry at him and understood why he had been away for so long. She wished he would have returned sooner, but that didn't matter now. After he set her down, Davia showed her the slippers from Dr. Sarnic, which she was happy to receive. She pulled them onto her feet as quickly as she could, as her feet were starting to actually feel cold.

"Do you like them? They're from Dr. Sarnic," Davia informed her. "I missed you very much, Princess," he added without realizing it.

Dorkla looked delighted. "You remembered the new name I was given," she happily answered. Looking down at her feet, she added, "Yes, I love them very much, Father, and I missed you. I kept waiting, but I knew you'd come. So what was prison like? Was it fun?"

Davia put his arm around Dorkla. "Let me tell you, baby girl. It was no picnic at the beach, if you know what I mean," he said with a sigh.

She looked eagerly up at him. "Did you find a cure for me yet so I can live a normal life again?" she asked hopefully.

Davia sighed again. "Sadly no. I haven't gotten another chance to ask that man yet. They snatched me away and put me in prison before I could get an answer." He stood up, reluctant to leave his lonely daughter. "I should probably get going on that right now." He turned and gave Dorkla a strong good-bye hug before leaving.

"Don't forget about me this time," Dorkla called after him. "Come and visit me again soon, okay?"

Chapter Twenty-Two

Search For a Cure

"I won't. I'll be back as soon as possible," Davia assured her. He turned and set off away from the freezing cave to go find the deaf-mute man in Kodaya.

Interestingly enough, this wasn't at all difficult to do, as the deaf-mute man was also looking for Davia. As he approached the area where he'd originally found the man, Davia saw him holding a large piece of parchment paper for Davia to read.

The man saw Davia and strode toward him, holding out the parchment and nodding his head. Davia snatched the parchment from his hand, unrolled it and read:

"I've been looking for you for the last few days. Where have you been?

Anyway, the cure is to destroy the ring. It must be broken into pieces to break the spell. That is all."

Davia was greatly relieved by this information. "Well, that should be easy. The ring is owned by a pawn-shop owner. I still have some money, enough to buy it," he said out loud, even though the man didn't hear it. He waved good-bye to the deaf-mute and set off for the pawn shop.

But once he entered the pawn shop and talked to the owner, his hopes fell. "I'm sorry, but I don't have the ring anymore," the owner informed him. "I sold it yesterday and can't remember who bought it."

Davia was devastated. This was his one and only chance to cure Dorkla, and now that possibility seemed ruined. What was he to do now? Unless he could find that ring, Dorkla would have to stay in her current state forever. He was beside himself with grief and frustration. He figured that the new owner of the ring didn't know of its power – or its ability to cause its wearer endless problems.

****

While Davia was agonizing over his daughter's potential fate, unbeknownst to him, the next day was going to be a special day for a little boy named Sanoma who lived in a little hut in the village of Cilowick where Dr. Sarnic lived. That day was his birthday, and he was turning six. He had already blown out the little candles and gotten several presents – mostly clothes, but no toys. Sanoma was disappointed until he saw there was one small package left. He picked it up and opened it as carefully as possible. What could it be? he thought, filled with the excitement of his special day. Getting impatient, he threw caution to the wind and tore open the package. Once opened, his face fell – it was a ring. "Just a stupid, lousy, dumb ring," he said in a disappointed voice. "I wanted toys!"

"Sanoma," his mother gently chided, "how could you say that about Aunt Milda's gift? It's the thought that counts."

"I don't blame him, Mother," Sanoma's sister chimed in. "I'd want toys if it was my birthday."

Thinking quickly, Aunt Milda gently said, "But dear, it is a toy when you wear it. It becomes a magical ring, giving you special powers."

"Really?" Sanoma asked, his face brightening. "Then I guess I like it after all!" He scampered off happily, admiring his new ring.

Sanoma's mother moved close to Aunt Milda and quietly said, "Now don't go putting crazy ideas in his head. You know very well there's nothing magical about that ring you gave him."

"I know that," Aunt Milda calmly replied, "but Sanoma doesn't. So what he doesn't know won't hurt him." Looking back at Sanoma, she added, "Besides, look how delighted he is with his present now."

****

His heart heavy, Davia decided to pay Dorkla another visit and deliver the bad news to her. It was not something he wanted to tell her, to admit that he had failed in his effort to find her a cure. Stepping into the cave, he got a chill, realizing how cold it really was in there. Seeing her father, Dorkla rushed over to him with a hopeful look on her face. "Papa, you're back! That was quick. So did you find out what my cure is?"

Davia couldn't bring himself to look at her as he answered slowly, "About that. You don't really need it by now, do you? You're probably getting used to it, adapting to cold climate. It's getting close to winter, you could come visit."

Dorkla's face fell. "Are you saying there's no cure after all? I guess I'm stuck in this fragile body of mine for life?" she cried out.

Davia reached out to touch her shoulder. "No, don't talk like that." he gently replied. There is hope. To cure you, all I have to do is destroy the ring."

"Then hurry up and go to the pawnshop," Dorkla demanded impatiently. "What are you waiting for?"

Davia sighed deeply before he replied, "I'm waiting for a different solution. They sold the ring yesterday."

"Then all we have to do is find out who has it now," Dorkla stated. "I need to go home and sleep in my bed, where it's warm and cozy."

Davia stood up. "I'll see you tomorrow," he told her as he turned to leave.

"Just don't give up on me, Father," Dorkla called after him. "I'll be waiting!"

At the cave entrance, Davia turned and smiled at her. "I won't. Now get some rest. Good-night!"

As he walked into the cool night air, he heard her call after him, "I will!"

Her final words echoed in the empty, cold cave. Things did feel hopeless now to Dorkla. She felt lonely in the cold air even though she wasn't affected by the chilly cave.

Davia was correct about it being almost winter because it was getting colder outsides as he headed for the castle, so much so that he could see his breath in white puffs.

He was in for a surprise upon entering the castle, as he could tell was alone no longer. There were candles lit in several rooms, he noticed as he looked around in surprise. "Do you like what I've done to the place, darling?" he heard a woman's voice call out. He followed the sound of her voice to the Throne Room, where he saw her sitting on the throne.

Davia's face froze in astonishment, as he found himself staring at a woman who looked like Amelia. "Who are you? What are you doing here?" he managed to finally gasp out. "I thought you were dead!"

"Let's just say I'm back from the dead," she purred. Seeing his look of disbelief, she added, "I'm kidding. I'm far from dead and never was to begin with. I'm not Amelia, but I am her twin sister, Ada. I like to think of myself as the evil twin, so to speak. I've come to reclaim her throne in case she ever passed away, which I heard she did." Rising up from the throne, evil Queen Ada saucily stated, "I found out that you killed her and got away free as a bird."

"I didn't know that Amelia had a twin – she never told me," Davia stated defensively. "Why are you here? You can't stay, this isn't your castle – it belongs to me!"

"I don't think so, according to Amelia's last will and testament in her diary," Queen Ada calmly replied. "It's all mine, including the rest of the money I took back while you were asleep," tossing the diary at his feet for him to read.

Davia bent down and picked up the diary. Looking at it, despite his rising anger he stated evenly, "What does this prove buit that you're a thief? I won't let someone like you stay here."

"Oh, we're staying, that's for sure," Queen Ada said silkily, twirling some of the gold coins in her hands. "As for why I'm here, it also involves getting you back and avenging Amelia's death."

"So that's it. You're planning on killing me. If it's just the money you want, you can keep it," Davia replied angrily, dropping the diary onto the floor.

Queen Ada's smile chilled Davia more than the ice cave could. "No, that would be too easy to just take your life. Amelia loved you, so I couldn't do that. But I can do what she did, which is to make you my slave. Then maybe someday soon, I can force you to help me make a baby."

"I don't think so. I'm nobody's slave, at least not anymore!" Davia shouted.

"Don't you see, Davia, you have no choice," Queen Ada said, smiling even more evilly than before. "You will always be in your room, and my guards" – at this point, she gestured to some men standing in the shadows – "will make sure of it. You'll eat when I feed you, and that will be the end of it. As it will soon be the end of the villages, because I will send them a message by burning their homes to the ground to let them know there's a new queen in town who demands respect." She let out a coldhearted laugh.

"How could you do such a thing?" Davia cried out in disgust. "The people will have no place to live. Dr. Sarnic lives in one of the villages, and we're friends now. You only care about yourself!"

"Exactly. Who am I supposed to care about? You're a murderer. I don't think so," Queen Ada replied with disdain in her voice. Gesturing to the guards, they went to Davia. Seizing him, they took Davia to his room to stay, which had been Dorkla's room. They found his bundle of clothes from when he'd first arrived at the castle and gave them to him, as he could not wear Dorkla's.

Once alone, Davia thought about his options. He went to the window, thinking that maybe he could jump down, but in his absence, he discovered that they had put bars on it. He could see that the guards were taking turns guarding the only door, so he couldn't escape that way. Sighing, he realized there was nothing he could do for the time being but get some sleep, which was what he had planned on doing until he'd arrived at the castle and discovered the fiasco this new evil queen had created.

When morning came, the queen sent her henchmen out on horses to warn the first village to be destroyed, which happened to be Cilowick. Upon approaching the town square in Cilowick, one of the guards dismounted and handed a scroll to one of the townsfolk, telling him in a gruff voice, "Make sure that everyone gets this message." Leaping back onto his horse, the guards turned their horses and headed back to the castle.

As he awoke and remembered what had happened last night, Davia felt like he was in prison all over again. He heard footsteps on the stone stairs, but it was only one of the guards bringing him his breakfast. It was nothing special, just some eggs, a hunk of bread and a cup of milk. He looked at it and sighed. Maybe with all that money she now has that she would have gotten him some meat. Then again, he couldn't complain. He was lucky that they gave him anything.

It didn't take very long at all for everyone in Cilowick to find out what the scroll said. As they leaned over to peer at it, they read:

"BY ORDER OF THE NEW QUEEN ADA – TOMORROW, ALL HOMES WILL BE DEMOLISHED. THOSE THAT FAIL TO COMPLY WILL BE BURNED ALONG WITH THEIR HOME. A REFUGEE CAMP WILL BE MADE AVAILABLE TO THOSE WHO OBEY. SINCERELY, YOUR NEW QUEEN, ADA."

"I don't know who she thinks she is, but I'm not leaving," said one villager.

"Are you crazy? She'll burn you alive along with your house," Dr. Sarnic stated. "I'm ready to leave. I've got my bags already packed."

Outside their homes, the villagers were busily talking to each other. "Somebody's got to do something," one said.

"All right everybody, back into your homes!" shouted someone above the crowd. Everyone agreed and complied.

"We can't just let this queen walk all over us. Somebody's got to stand up to her and fight back," Sanoma insisted.

"We have no choice," said his mother.

"But Mother, where are we going to live? I've been here my whole life," Sanoma stated, fighting back tears.

Sighing, his mother replied, "Wherever the refugee camp will be, I guess." A short while later, declaring a need for some more rest, his mother went to her room to get some more sleep. Once he knew she was soundly asleep, Sanoma left their hut in search of help.

****

Dorkla woke up and stretched her legs, realizing that it must be near midday. Shouldn't Father have visited me by now, she wondered to herself. She hoped that he had found the ring so she could leave the cave. Maybe I could leave soon, she thought. It's getting colder outside of the cave. It couldn't be that harmful, could it? Before she could think anymore, she was startled by the sound of footsteps nearby. Could it possibly be her father? The sound got closer until a small figure entered the cave. "Who goes there?" Dorkla shouted, as her voice echoed through the cave.

A small voice replied, "Sorry, I didn't think anyone lived here. I used to play in this cave a lot. I forgot to introduce myself. I'm Sanoma, and who are you?"

Chapter Twenty-Three

The Final Showdown

Remembering her manners now that she was no longer frightened by her visitor, Dorkla reached out her hand to shake his and answered, "I'm pleased to meet you. You can call me Dorkla." As she shook his hand, she noticed the ring on his finger and added, "That's a nice ring you have there."

Sanoma's face brightened. "You really like it? I got it as a gift for my birthday," he stated proudly, holding up his hand for her to see.

"Yes, it's marvelous," Dorkla replied. "Could I have it? I'll give you a... kiss on the lips in exchange."

Sanoma turned away from her, holding his hand against his stomach. "No, you can't have it. Like I said, it's a present from my aunt. I can't just give it away. Besides, girls have cooties. And it gives me magical powers."

"How did you know?" Dorkla asked in surprise. "I guess if you don't want to give it to me, then there's nothing I can do. So then," she went on," why are you here? Are you hiding from someone?"

Sanoma slowly took the ring off and put it in his left shirt pocket. "But I don't think it works. I don't feel any differently. No, I'm not hiding at all. I'm looking for someone to help me stop the evil queen that lives in the castle."

"You mean *my* castle. I thought only my father was living there. That explains why he hasn't come and visited me." Dorkla looked troubled.

"It goes like this. The evil Queen Ada today said she's burning down our villages. That is, unless I can stop her, but I can't do it alone. That's why I'm looking for help. Unfortunately, all I could find was you, a scrawny little girl," Sanoma declared petulantly.

"What do you mean by that?" Dorkla asked angrily. "I'm not just a girl! I can get the job done!"

"So you'll do it then?" Sanoma asked hopefully, excitement rising in his voice.

"Not now that you've hurt my feelings, I won't" Dorkla said in a hurt tone.

"Come on, please?" Sanoma begged. "I'll do anything! Just name it."

"Okay then, give me your ring and we have a deal," Dorkla demanded.

Sanoma's face fell. "But I told you, it was a gift," he protested. Seeing her unyielding expression, he added, "Okay, fine, you win. Here you go," as he dug the ring out of his pocket and grudgingly handed it to her.

"Thank you! You won't regret this," Dorkla stated happily. She quickly decided to hang onto it and not destroy it yet. She also decided it best to leave at night so it would be colder and less of a chance of her dying. They used this time to devise a plan of what they would do when they got there. Once they both had the plan down and memorized, Dorkla ate her midday meal, which she shared with Sanoma. This consisted of frozen fruit and cold precooked fish, as these things were easily thawed, unlike some of the other items Dr. Sarnic had stored in the cave. The only really warm items were the hot meals Dr. Sarnic would bring over from home, carefully wrapped to stay as warm as possible on his trips to the cave.

While Dorkla's thoughts were on Dr. Sarnic, she was startled when he suddenly appeared in the cave, only this time he had all of his belongings with him. "Dr. Sarnic, what are *you* doing here?" she asked.

"Oh, I'm sorry to ask, but can I stay here awhile?" Dr. Sarnic asked in a sad voice. "I have nowhere to go. The queen's planning on burning down my house, so I won't be able to stay there any longer."

"It's okay for you to stay for a little while. You won't have to be here for long," Dorkla answered assuringly. "You'll get to go back to your home soon. Sanoma and I are going to stop that evil Queen Ada from destroying the village."

Feeling somewhat comforted by her words, Dr. Sarnic eagerly asked, "Can I help, please? I know you probably don't want an old man like me getting in the way."

"No, don't be silly," Dorkla stated with a smile. "You can hang around. You might be able to be of some use. We still need someone to carry the things we'll use and hold onto them."

"I'll try my best, because I still want to keep my home," Dr. Sarnic promised.

"Well, we can't leave just yet though. It's not cold enough outside," Dorkla stated. "So we're going to have to pass the time somehow."

"I'm sure we might find something to do in the meantime," Dr. Sarnic said smiling. Turning to Sanoma, he asked, "Sanoma, shouldn't you be at home at this time?"

"I have to leave my home, too," Sanoma said defiantly. "So I'll need Dorkla to help me stop Queen Ada."

"Don't say that, calling her a queen," Dorkla demanded. "She's not one. Just because she walks into our castle and declares herself one!"

"Oh, I forgot to give you this," Dr. Sarnic said absently, pulling out a carefully-wrapped parcel of food from his bag. "I was planning on saving this for later, but why not now?" He retrieved a loaf of bread, broke it into pieces and gave some to Dorkla and some to Sanoma.

Dorkla took a bite and said, "It's pretty good. Better than the frozen food in this cave!"

While they were finishing, Dorkla thought maybe it was cold enough that they could leave. It would probably be dark by the time they walked to their destination. Once everyone was done with their bread, Dorkla stated, "Let's get going, everybody!" Sanoma nodded his assent.

On the way there, they chatted eagerly about what they were about to do. "Do you have the plan memorized, Sanoma?" Dorkla asked.

"Sure do," Sanoma replied confidently, "It won't be a problem. I'm sure everything will go smoothly."

"What plan are you speaking of?" Dr. Sarnic queried. "I wasn't told about any plan. What am I going to be doing?"

"You'll find out when we get there," Dorkla answered mysteriously.

By this time, they had reached Cilowick. Sanoma stated, "There's my house where I live. Should I tell my mother where I'm going or what I'm going to do?"

"No, that won't be necessary," Dorkla replied. "You don't want to make her worry. Besides, we don't have time."

"What are you talking about? We have plenty of time!" Sanoma insisted.

"No, we don't," Dorkla stated firmly. "I can't be outside for too long. It's not cold enough. Plus, don't you want to put an end to Ada's plans? I can't keep my father waiting. He's counting on me freezing him from her clutches." Sanoma nodded in understanding, and they continued on.

As they arrived in Kodaya, Dorkla said, "I guess we found a way to pass the time because it's getting dark out now." Passing by the shops that were closing for the night, they could see the castle up ahead.

"Only a little more to go and we'll be there," Dorkla stated. Before they reached the castle, Dorkla, who had assumed the role of leader of the group, told everyone to be quiet and only whisper. At last, they approached the castle.

****

Davia was still up in his room trying to stay sane and patient. "I'm starting to think Amelia was a saint compared to this," he grumbled, scraping his cup back and forth on the bars across the window.

"Be quiet up there!" a guard barked out.

****

The reason they had to be quiet was obvious. They couldn't let anyone know they were there, or they would be caught. They also did not want to wake up the guards who were sleeping. They crept past the front guard, who was barely awake and nodding off just in time for them to pass by without being noticed. They went first to the shed to get supplies consisting of a bucket and a rope. Dr. Sarnic was handed both of these items and instructed to guard both Dorkla and Sanoma if they needed help in times of trouble.

"I don't know what you have planned to use these things, but I hope your plan works out, Dorkla," Dr. Sarnic whispered to her. "I'll stand by when needed."

The first objective in Dorkla's plan was to take out the front guard. To accomplish this, Dr. Sarnic gave Dorkla the bucket. She quietly put water in the bucket from the one in the well until it was more than half-full. She instructed Sanoma to get far in front of the guard while Dorkla held onto the bucket, standing somewhat near the guard. Remembering his role in the this part of the plan, Sanoma caused a distraction, making a diversion by jumping up and down and yelling, "Hey you, you big turkey! Come and get me!"

It worked, because the guard woke up. Once he realized the cause of the noise, he started after Sanoma, who began running. He stopped when he saw Dorkla dumped the water on the ground, where it began to pool around his feet. He turned around and laughed, "You think some water's gonna stop me, little girl?" Setting the bucket down, Dorkla bent down and touched the ground. The guard tried to make a grab for her, but her touch froze the water, making a solid sheet of ice upon which the guard slipped and slid in the nick of time. They thought that his fall would knock the guard unconscious; however, he started to struggle to regain his feet. At least he was until he was knocked out by a blow to his head from a shovel wielded by Dr. Sarnic.

"Sorry kids, you can never be sure," said Dr. Sarnic with a grin. He handed the rope to Sanoma, who tied one end around his waist and carried the rest of its length as he went into the castle.

Queen Ada was sitting on her throne, and espying the little boy, she said with a sneer, "Look what the cat dragged in! Well, if my guard didn't stop you, I will." She got up and went after him. This gave Dorkla more than enough time to sneak into the castle past Ada and the guard, who was so exhausted he fell asleep due to staying awake guarding Davia.

Guessing where her father was kept, she rushed up the stairs to her room. Davia was filled with joy upon seeing his daughter. Dorkla leapt into his arms, giving him a big hug while he held her tightly. "I missed you so much, honey, I thought I'd never see you again!" Davia said, while tears filled his eyes.

"We're going to get you out of here, Father!" Dorkla cried.

Releasing her from his arms, Davia looked at her with amazement and asked, "How did you get here?"

"Oh, just with a little help from a boy named Sanoma and Dr. Sarnic," she happily answered.

Downstairs, the chase was still in progress. Ada was running after Sanoma around the table almost to the point of making them both dizzy. Suddenly, Sanoma went under the table. Ada ducked her head to see and hit her head on the side of the table. She staggered from the pain, holding the palm of her hand to her head. This opportunity gave Sanoma enough time to bite her ankle, and she collapsed onto the stone floor. Sanoma grabbed the rope from around his waist and quickly tied her up.

When Dorkla and her father came down the stairs, Dorkla saw what Sanoma had done. "Good job, Sanoma!" she exclaimed with delight. The boy grinned at her.

They thought they were in the clear, but the sleeping guard had awakened from hearing all the noise. Coming into the Throne Room, he was about to stop them, but for reason he did not. He looked outside, saw the unconscious guard and Ada tied up. She looked up, saw him and screamed, "Stop them, you bumbling idiot fool!"

The guard gave her a steely look and told her, "I'm done taking orders from you. I'm going to get some more sleep!" Realizing her full defeat, she laid down on the floor.

When the victorious group stepped outside the castle, there was a massive crowd of villagers lingering outside. Dorkla spotted Mia and Caleb among the large group and smiled happily at them. The villagers wanted Ada out of the castle once and for all. Davia went back into the castle, picked up Ada and marched her outside, while Dorkla also dragged the sleeping guard outside.

"The queen has been defeated!" Davia announced. "You can have her. There will be no more taxes from now on!" He lifted Dorkla high up in his arms as the crowd cheered wildly. "All I need is my daughter!" The angry mob descended upon Ada and her henchmen and carried them off to make sure they'd never bring harm to this country again.

"I guess that everything is now done and taken care of," Davia joyfully stated to Dorkla as he set her down on the ground.

"Not yet, Father," she replied, looking up at him. "There's something else left I need to do."

"What's that?"

"You'll see," Dorkla answered with a mysterious smile. Dorkla headed to the shed, with Davia right behind her. She pulled a hammer from its placed in the shed and went over to a tree stump nearby. Quickly dipping the ring in a bucket of water, Dorkla placed the ring in the middle of the stump. She then touched the ring with a finger, freezing it solid but making it brittle. Raising the hammer up high, she struck the ring with a strong blow, breaking it into many pieces.

Turning to her father, she said to him, "Now it is finished."

ISBN 141208978-6